W9-BBV-661
WITHDRAWN
FROM THE RODMAN PUBLIC LIBRARY

LAST RESPECTS

By Catherine Aird

LAST RESPECTS
PASSING STRANGE
SOME DIE ELOQUENT
PARTING BREATH
SLIGHT MOURNING
HIS BURIAL TOO
A LATE PHOENIX
THE STATELY HOME MURDER
HENRIETTA WHO?
A MOST CONTAGIOUS GAME
THE RELIGIOUS BODY

LAST RESPECTS

CATHERINE AIRD, *pseud.*

PUBLISHED FOR THE CRIME CLUB BY
DOUBLEDAY & COMPANY, INC.
GARDEN CITY, NEW YORK
1982

RODMAN PUBLIC LIBRARY

38212005932998
Main Adult Mystery
Aird, C
Aird, Catherine
Last respects

All of the characters in this book
are fictitious, and any resemblance
to actual persons, living or dead,
is purely coincidental.

The chapter headings are taken from
The Beggar's Opera by John Gay.

Library of Congress Cataloging in Publication Data

Aird, Catherine, pseud.
Last respects.

I. Title.
PR6051.I65L3 1982 823'.914
ISBN 0-385-18256-2 AACR2
Library of Congress Catalog Card Number 82–45344

First Edition in the United States of America

Copyright © 1982 by Catherine Aird
All Rights Reserved
Printed in the United States of America

Acknowledgment

Michael Burnham, ship scientist

Ma plume pour toutes mes tantes.

CHAPTER 1

Suspicion does not become a friend.

The man wasn't alive and well and living in Paris.

He wasn't living in the county of Calleshire, England, either.

And he certainly wasn't alive and well. Actually he wasn't living anywhere. He was dead. Obviously dead.

Horace Boller was so sure about that that he didn't hurry after he had seen him. Not that Horace Boller was the hurrying sort. In addition to which he was out fishing at the time and fishermen never hurry. It was a universal truth. You couldn't catch fish if you hurried. The fish didn't like it: they stopped feeding at once. Like primitive man, fish equated hurry with danger and either kept their heads down or made off. In Horace Boller's considered opinion civilised man had a lot to learn about hurrying.

As it happened Boller hadn't so much seen the dead man at first as just caught a quick glimpse of something out of the ordinary in the water. It took his brain a moment or two to sort out the message from his eye: that that which was floating beyond the bow of his boat and just out of range of easy vision could be a body. He wedged his fishing rod so that he had a spare hand and reached for one of the oars. He gave it a purposive poke and the rowing boat obediently came round so that he was a little nearer to what was in the water.

It was after that that he had ceased to be in any real doubt about what it was he was looking at. The body was floating just under the surface of the water in the way that bodies did, arms outstretched. It was apparently moving. Horace Boller was not deceived. It was, he knew at once, totally lifeless. The illusion of movement came from the water, not from the man. It was one of the tricks—the many tricks—that water played. The angle of refraction came into it, too. Boller didn't know anything about angles of refraction but he did know a lot about the tricks that water could play.

This man had been dead for quite a while. He knew that, too, at once. That conclusion was not reached as a result of a long acquaintance with dead bodies—although Horace Boller had seen some of those in his time too—but from something indefinable about the appearance of the body even at a distance.

If you were to ask him, his considered opinion would be that it had been in the water a fair old time.

There was, of course, no one about to ask him that—or anything else. It was precisely because there was no one about that Horace Boller had chosen to come out fishing today. You couldn't catch fish when the water wasn't quiet. He looked about him now. There wasn't even one other boat in sight let alone within hailing distance. That was because it was a Tuesday. Now if it had been a weekend he would hardly have been able to get his boat out into the main channel of the river for yachts and sailing dinghies.

It was this indefinable sense that this particular body had been in the water for more than a little while that made Horace Boller dismiss the idea of taking it in tow.

Well, that—and something else as well . . .

The Boller family had been around in Calleshire for a long time. Not quite in the same well-documented way that His Grace the Duke of Calleshire had been at Calle Castle but for pretty nearly the same length of time. There had certainly been Bollers living in the little fishing village of Edsway on the estuary of the River Calle for as long as anyone had bothered to look. Those who looked didn't include the Bollers. They had better things to do than go searching through old parish records—things like building boats, running ferries, making sails, digging for bait at low tide . . .

The tide still mattered in Edsway. Once upon a time—in the

dim past when all boats had had a shallow draught—Edsway had been the only port on the estuary. It was always something of a natural harbour, sheltered by a lip of headland from the worst of the storms coming in from the sea—the village of Marby juxta Mare took the brunt of those—but there had never been really deep water at Edsway and now—thanks to the sand—there was less.

Its commercial fate had been sealed in the nineteenth century when some distant railway baron had decreed that Mr. Stephenson's newfangled iron road should go from Calleford to the river mouth and thus to the sea on the other—the north side—of the river. That was when Kinnisport had come into prominence and Edsway fallen into desuetude. In the wake of the railway had come another entrepreneur who had caused a proper deep water harbour to be built at Kinnisport out of great blocks of granite shipped down by sea from Aberdeen—and Edsway had dropped out of the prosperity race altogether.

But only for the time being.

Every dog did have its day.

Now it was Kinnisport that was in decline while Edsway was enjoying a twentieth-century revival as a sailing centre. The firm sand that had choked its life as a commercial harbour provided an excellent basis for the hardstanding that the little boats needed and some safe swimming for their owners' families.

The dead man hadn't been a bather.

You didn't go swimming in a shirt and trousers. Not voluntarily, that is.

Horace Boller took another look at the man floating in the water. He might have been a seaman, he might not. The Calleshire shore got its share of those drowned on the high seas and the village of Edsway got more than its quota of them. It had something to do with the configuration of the coast and the way in which the tide came up the estuary to meet the River Calle coming down to the sea.

Bodies usually fetched up on the spit of land known locally as Billy's Finger. This stretched out into the water and—so the experts said—each year got a little shallower on the seaward side and a little deeper on the river side. The river scoured away from behind what the sea laid up at its front. The ancients used to say that Billy's Finger moved, that it beckoned mariners to their doom. The moderns—the clever ones who knew everything because a computer had worked it out for them—had said, rather surprised, that the ancients were right after all. Billy's Finger did move. It moved about an inch every hundred years, a little more at the very tip.

Horace Boller took a bearing from the spire of St. Peter's Church and reckoned that this fellow, whoever he was, had for once somehow escaped the beckonings of Billy's Finger. And he had done that in spite of its being the season of neap tides. Boller wasn't too bothered about that. These days it didn't make any difference exactly whereabouts a dead body found landfall. He would still—unless claimed by sorrowing relatives—end up buried in St. Peter's churchyard at Edsway. There he—whoever he was—would lie in the goodly company of all those other unknown men who had been washed up by the sea.

Some had unmarked graves and some had those that were dignified by tombstones. There was a melancholy row betokening a remote naval engagement far out to sea in 1917. All those memorials bore the same inscription "A Sailor of the Great War—Known unto God." They hadn't even heard the distant thunder of the guns in Edsway but the men had come ashore.

In the end.

It hadn't always been like that.

Once upon a time when drowned men had been washed ashore on Billy's Finger the men of Edsway had seen to it that they weren't found and brought to land for burial in St. Peter's churchyard. They had, in fact, taken very good care that they weren't. Some antiquarian who had taken an interest in the estuary's local history had once told Horace Boller all about it.

The villagers in those days had felt that they had a big enough Poor Rate to cope with as it was without taking on the cost—as a charge upon it—of burying unknown seamen. What they used to do in olden times, this antiquarian had told an impassive Horace Boller, was to wait for nightfall and then drag the body over from the seaward aspect of the strand and lower it into the deep water the other side of Billy's Finger.

The combination of sea and river—tide and current—saw to it then that the next landfall of the dead body was in the neighbouring parish of Collerton. And thus it became a charge on their Poor Rate instead.

Horace Boller had listened unblinkingly to this recital, saying, "Well, I never!" at suitable intervals, as he knew you had to do with this manner of man. Privately he had considered it an excellent way of keeping the rates down and hadn't doubted that there would have been Bollers in the clandestine non-burial party.

"The Overseers of the Poor doubtless turned a blind eye," said the antiquarian. He prided himself on having what he thought was a good knowledge of the seamy side of human nature. That went with a study of the past.

"I daresay," said Horace Boller, whose own knowledge went a little deeper, "that they were glad to have it done."

"Well, yes, but the law was . . ."

Horace Boller had only listened with half an ear at the time. The letter of the law wasn't one of his yardsticks. Besides he himself had found the careful study of the official mind a more rewarding business than history.

"They'd be more at home in Collerton churchyard anyway," he had said to the antiquarian, who by then was beginning to come between Horace and the job he happened to have on hand at the time.

"Pardon?" The antiquarian had known a lot but he hadn't known everything.

"The north-west corner of Collerton churchyard floods every time the river rises," Horace had taken pleasure in informing him. "Didn't you know that?"

What Horace Boller was thinking about now, out on the water and with an actual body in view, wasn't exactly the same as pushing a financial liability into the next parish but it came very near to it. What he was considering was the best move to make next—the best move from the point of view of Horace Boller, citizen and occasional taxpayer, that is.

He steadied the oars in the rowlocks and considered the state of the tide. He was always conscious of it but particularly when he was out on the water. It wasn't far off the turn and he certainly wasn't going to row a body back to Edsway against the tide. The reasoning sped glibly through his mind as he took enough bearings to mark the spot in the water where the body was floating. Already he heard himself saying, "I couldn't lift it aboard myself, of course, Mr. Ridgeford. Not on my own like. I couldn't tow it back either. Not against the tide . . . not without help. I'm not as young as I used to be, you know . . ."

Half an hour later he was using just those very words to Police Constable Ridgeford. Brian Ridgeford was young enough to be Horace Boller's son but Horace still deemed it politic to call him "Mister." This approach was one of the fruits of his study of the ways of the official mind.

"Dead, you said?" checked Constable Ridgeford, reaching for his telephone.

"Definitely dead," said Horace. He'd taken off his cap when he stepped into the constable's little office and he stood there now with it dangling from his hand as if he were already a mourner.

"How did you know it was a man?" asked Ridgeford.

The question didn't trouble Horace Boller. "Floating on its back," he said.

"I'll have to report it to Headquarters," said Ridgeford importantly, beginning to dial. A body made a change from dealing with old Miss Finch, who—difficult and dogmatic—insisted that there were Unidentified Flying Objects on the headland behind Marby.

"That's right," said Horace.

Ridgeford frowned. "There may be someone missing."

"So there may."

"Not that I've heard of anyone." The constable pulled a pile of reports on his desk forward and started thumbing through them with one hand while he held the telephone in the other.

"Nor me," said Horace at once. It had been one of the factors that had weighed with him when he decided not to bring the body in. It hadn't been someone local or he would have heard. "But then . . ."

Ridgeford's attitude suddenly changed. He stiffened and almost came to attention. "Is that F Division Headquarters at Berebury? This is Constable Ridgeford from Edsway reporting . . ."

Horace Boller waited patiently for the outcome.

A minute or two later he heard Ridgeford say, "Just a moment, sir, and I'll ask the fisherman who reported it. He'll know." The young constable covered the mouthpiece of the telephone with his free hand and said to Horace, "Where will that body fetch up if it's left in the water?"

Boller screwed up his face and thought quickly. "Hard to say exactly, Mr. Ridgeford. Most probably," he improvised, "under the cliffs over on the Kinnisport side of the estuary." He waved an arm. "You know, where the rocks stick out into the water. Not," he added, "for a couple of days, mind you."

He stepped back, well pleased with himself. What he had just said to the policeman was a complete fabrication from start to finish. Left to itself the body of the dead man might continue on its course up river to Collerton for the length of a tide or two but then either the change in the tide or the river current would pick it up and bring it back downstream again. Then the timeless eddies of the sea would lay it up on Billy's Finger as they had always done since time began.

Constable Ridgeford, though, did not know this. He was young, he was new in Edsway and, most importantly of all, he was from the town. In towns water came in pipes.

"H'm," he said. "You're sure about that, are you?"

"Certain," said Boller, although the rocks under the cliff near Cranberry Point were a long way from where he had last seen the dead man. They just happened to be the most inaccessible and inconvenient place on the coast from which to attempt to recover a body that Horace could think of on the spur of the moment.

"They'd have to take it up the cliff-face on a cradle from there, wouldn't they?" said Ridgeford, frowning.

"Oh, yes," said Boller at once. "You'd never get a recovery boat to land on those rocks. Too dangerous. Mind you," he added craftily, "the coastguards up top would probably spot it for you easily enough."

"Er—yes, of course," said Ridgeford.

Horace Boller said nothing but he knew he'd played a trump card. Another of the fruits of his study of the official mind was the sure and certain knowledge that owners of them did not relish cooperation with other official services. Over the years the playing off of one department against another had become a high art with the wily old fisherman.

Ridgeford turned back to the telephone and had further speech with his superior. That officer must have put another question to him because once again Ridgeford covered the mouthpiece. "You marked the spot with a buoy, didn't you?"

"Sorry, Mr. Ridgeford," lied Horace fluently, "I didn't happen to have one with me. I was just out to catch something for my tea, that's all."

There were six orange marker buoys in the locker of Horace's rowing boat. He would have to make quite sure that the constable didn't see them.

"I took proper bearings though, Mr. Ridgeford," said Boller.

"You mean you could take me out there?"

"If my son came too," said Horace cunningly. "I reckon we could get him aboard and back to dry land, whoever he is, in no time at all."

"I'll meet you on the slipway in twenty minutes," said the constable briskly.

"Right you are, Mr. Ridgeford." Horace replaced his cap and turned to go.

"And," the policeman added drily, "I'll bring my own rope just in case you were thinking we ought to get a new one from Hopton's."

Hopton's was the ship's-chandler on Shore Street. It was the store where the myriad of small boat owners bought the necessities of weekend sailing. Mrs. Hopton had been a Boller before she married.

"Just as you say, Mr. Ridgeford," said Horace. He felt no rancour: on the contrary. Like Alexander Solzhenitsyn's hero Ivan Denisovich, he was a great one for counting his blessings. As a little later he settled his oars comfortably in the rowlocks while his son pushed the boat off from the slipway, he even felt a certain amount of satisfaction. There would be a fee to come from Her Majesty's Coroner for the County of Calleshire for assisting in the recovery of the drowned man and that fee would only have to be shared within the family.

Police Constable Brian Ridgeford settled himself in the bow and looked steadily forward, his thoughts following a different tack. He wasn't a fool and he hadn't been in Edsway long, but long enough to learn some of the little ways of the Boller tribe. He had not been entirely deceived by Horace's manoeuvres either. He had been well aware, too, that when he, Brian Ridgeford, had dropped in on Ted Boller, carpenter and undertaker for all the villages roundabout, on his way to the slipway, to warn him that there might be a body for him to convey to the mortuary in Berebury, this fact was not news to Ted Boller. It had been immediately apparent to the police constable that Horace had wasted no time in alerting Ted, who was Horace's cousin. Naturally Ted had not said anything to the policeman about this. While Horace was cunning, Ted was sly and he'd just promised to keep an eye open for the return of their boat and to be ready and waiting by the shore when they got back.

The two Bollers pulled steadily on their oars while Horace did some calculations about tide flow.

"Be about an hour and a bit since I left him, wouldn't it, Mr. Ridgeford?" he said.

"If you came straight to me," said the constable.

Boller turned his head to take a bearing from the spire of St. Peter's Church and another from the chimneys of Collerton House. "A bit farther," he said.

Both oarsmen bent to their task, while Constable Ridgeford scanned the water ahead.

Presently Horace turned his head again, this time to take in the state of the tide by looking across at the saltings. They were invisible at high water. Birds on them betokened low tide. "Turn her up river a bit more," he commanded.

Once they reached what Horace Boller thought was the right place the drowned man took surprisingly little time to locate. Brian Ridgeford spotted him first and the three men got him aboard without too much of a struggle. The victim of the water wasn't a big man. He had had dark hair and might have been any age at all. That was really all that Brian Ridgeford noted before he helped Horace cover him first with a black plastic bag and then with the tarpaulin that was doing duty as a temporary winding sheet.

Once on dry land and safely in the official care of the Calleshire Constabulary—although still with a member of the Boller family ready to put his thumb on a fee—the body made greater speed. Ted Boller and his undertaker's van soon set off towards Billing Bridge and Berebury. Strictly speaking it was Billing Bridge that marked the end of the estuary. Some medieval men had earned merit by building churches: if you couldn't build a church, then you built a bridge. Cornelius Billing had bought his way into the history and topography of the county of Calleshire in 1484 by building a bridge over the River Calle at the farthest point down river that it had been possible to build a bridge in 1484.

Ted Boller slowed his vehicle down as he bumped his way over it in a primitive tribute to his passenger, who was far beyond feeling anything at all, while Constable Ridgeford walked back to his own house, beginning to draft in his mind the details of his report. He wondered idly which day the coroner would nominate for the inquest . . .

Just as some men liked to toy with a chess problem so Police Constable Brian Ridgeford passed his walk considering whether he could summon a jury in Edsway—should the coroner want to sit with one, that is—without calling upon a single member of the vast Boller family to serve on it. Like countering one of the rarer chess gambits it would be difficult but he reckoned that it could be done.

Ted Boller's hearse duly delivered the unknown man to the mortuary presided over by Dr. Dabbe, Consultant Pathologist to the Berebury District Hospital Group. Such minimal paper-work that the body had so far acquired on its short journey from sea to land and from coast to town accompanied it and said briefly, "Found drowned."

"Found drowned, my foot," said the pathologist two minutes after looking at the body.

CHAPTER 2

The company are met.

"Found drowned, his foot," repeated Police Superintendent Leeyes not very long afterwards.

As soon as the pathologist's message had come through to Berebury Police Station he had summoned Detective Inspector C. D. Sloan to his office. Inspector Sloan—known as Christopher Dennis to his nearest and dearest—was for obvious reasons called "Seedy" by his friends. He was the head of Berebury's Criminal Investigation Department. It was a tiny department but such crime as there was in that corner of Calleshire usually landed up in Detective Inspector Sloan's lap.

In any case—in every case, you might say—Superintendent Leeyes always saw to it that nothing stayed on his own desk that could be delegated to someone else's. That desk was usually Sloan's.

"Found in water, though?" advanced Sloan, who was well-versed in his superior officer's little ways. He was a great one for passing the buck, was the superintendent.

Downwards.

Detective Inspector Sloan could never remember a problem being referred to a higher level—in their case the Headquarters of the County Constabulary at Calleford—if Superintendent Leeyes could possibly help it. Sloan was, though, well aware of—indeed, would never forget—some of those problems that the superintendent had in the past directed downwards to his own desk. A body found in water but not drowned sounded as if it might very well be another of the unforgettables.

"Brought in from the estuary," expanded Leeyes. "Someone reported it to Constable Ridgeford."

Sloan nodded. "Our man in Edsway."

"He's young," added the superintendent by way of extra identification.

Sloan nodded again. He wasn't talking about the body. Sloan knew that. The superintendent had meant the constable.

"Very young." The superintendent at the same time contrived to make youth sound like an indictment.

Sloan nodded his head in acknowledgement of this observation too. He even toyed with the idea of saying that they had all been young once—including the chief constable—but he decided against it. Medical students, he knew, when certain specific diseases were being taught, were always reminded that the admiral had once been a midshipman; the bishop, a curate . . . Anyway it was quite true that constables did seem to come in two sizes. Young and untried was one of them. Old and cunning was another. The trouble was that the first group had seen nothing and that the second lot—the oldies—had seen it all. The latter tended to be world-weary about everything except their own lack of promotion. On this subject, though, they were apt to wax very eloquent indeed . . .

"And," carried on Leeyes, "I don't know how much of a greenhorn Ridgeford is."

The only exception to the rule about old and disgruntled constables that Sloan knew was Constable Mason. He must be about due for retirement now—he'd been stationed over at Great Rooden for as long as anyone could remember. The trouble with Constable Mason from the hierarchy's point of view was that he had steadily declined promotion over the years. More heretical still, he had continually declared himself very well content with his lot.

"I don't," said Leeyes grumpily, "want to find out the hard way about Ridgeford."

"No, sir," said Sloan, his mind still on Mason. The bizarre attitude of that constable to his career prospects had greatly troubled Superintendent Leeyes. If the donkey does not want the carrot there is only the stick left—and there has to be a good reason for using that. Consequently a puzzled Police Superintendent Leeyes had always watched the crime rate out at Great Rooden with exceedingly close attention. Mason, however, was as good as any Mountie in getting his man. This, he said modestly, was because he had a head start when there was villainy about. He not only usually knew who had committed the crime but where to lay his hands on the culprit as well . . .

"Besides," complained Leeyes, "you've got to put the young men somewhere."

"Yes, sir," Sloan heartily agreed with that. "And some of them have got to go out into the country."

"As long as they don't take to growing cabbages," said Leeyes. Constable Mason—old Constable Mason—insisted that he liked living in the country. That was another of the things that had bothered the urban Superintendent Leeyes. Another was that there really seemed to be no crime to speak of in Great Rooden anyway. The superintendent had put the most sinister construction possible on the situation but three anti-corruption specialists—heavily disguised as government auditors—had failed to find Mason collaborating improperly with anyone.

"We can't," growled Superintendent Leeyes, his mind on Constable Ridgeford of Edsway, "keep them all here in Berebury tied to our apron strings, can we?"

"We can't keep an eye on them all the time even if we do," said Detective Inspector Sloan, who had ideas of his own about the "being thrown in the deep end" approach. "Besides, we're not wet nurses."

That had been a Freudian slip on Sloan's part and he regretted it at once.

"This body," said Leeyes on the instant, "was picked up in the water between Collerton and Edsway." He moved over from his desk to a vast map of the county of Calleshire which was fixed to the wall of his office. It clearly showed the estuary of the River Calle from Billing Bridge westwards down to the sea with Kinnisport standing sentinel on the north shore and Edsway sheltering under the headland on the southern edge, with the village of Marby juxta Mare over on the seacoast to the south-west. It was a contour map and the headland between Edsway and Marby called the Cat's Back showed up well.

The limits of F Division were heavily outlined in thick black pencil. Each time that he saw it Detective Inspector Sloan was reminded of the ground plan of a medieval fortress. Superintendent Leeyes added to the illusion by presiding over his territory with much the same outlook as a feudal baron.

He put his thumb on the map now. "They found it about here, upstream from Edsway."

"And downstream from Collerton." Detective Inspector Sloan made a note. "Is there anyone missing from hereabouts? I haven't heard of . . ."

"I've got someone pulling a list now," said Leeyes briskly, "and I've been on to the coastguards."

Sloan lifted his eyes towards the point on the map where the stretch of cliff beyond Kinnisport showed. "Ah, yes," he murmured, "they might know something, mightn't they?"

It was the wrong thing to say.

"It all depends on how wide awake they are," sniffed Leeyes.

"Quite so," said Sloan.

"I don't see myself," said the superintendent heavily, "how anyone can keep an eye on them out on the cliffs like that."

"Still, they might have seen something."

"It's too quiet by half up there," pronounced Leeyes.

"That's true," agreed Sloan. Mercifully Cranberry Point did not have the attractions of Beachy Head. He was profoundly thankful that those who wished to end it all did not often buy single tickets to Kinnisport and walk out to the cliffs. The rocks at the bottom were singularly uninviting. Today's victim wasn't likely to be a suicide: not if he was found in the water but not drowned . . .

"The trouble," declared Leeyes, still harping on the coastguards, "is that nothing ever happens up there on the cliff to keep them on their toes."

"No, sir," agreed Sloan. The superintendent was a great believer in a constant state of alert. In an earlier age he would have been a notable success as a performer with a dancing bear. It would have been on its toes, all right. "This chap could have been a seaman, I suppose."

"Eight bells," said Leeyes suddenly.

"Pardon, sir?"

"Sunset and rise and shine," said Leeyes.

"Er—quite so, sir."

"The old watch stands down, duty done," intoned Leeyes sonorously. "The new watch takes over."

"The coastguards'll know about shipping, surely though, sir?" Sloan ventured back onto firmer ground.

"Ah," said Leeyes, unwilling to impute any merit at all to a distinguished service, "that depends if their records are any good or not, doesn't it?"

"I suppose it does." Sloan wasn't going to argue: with anyone else, perhaps, but not with Superintendent Leeyes and not at the very beginning of a case.

"Remember," said Leeyes darkly, "that not everything gets reported. Especially at sea."

There was no thick black line extending F Division out into the sea to the territorial limit but in Leeyes's view there should have been. From time to time he hankered after the autocratic authority of the captain of a ship at sea as well.

"They'll listen in all the time to radio messages at sea, though," pointed out Sloan. "Bound to."

He didn't know about nothing being sacred any longer but he did know that between radio and computer nothing much remained secret for very long.

"All right, all right," conceded Leeyes. "They may have picked something up. We'll have to wait and see what they say."

Detective Inspector Sloan kept his mind on essentials. "But it isn't a case of drowning, you say, sir?"

"Not me, Sloan," countered Leeyes robustly. "I didn't say any such thing. It's the pathologist who says that."

"Ah."

"And I don't suppose he'll change his mind either. You know what Dr. Dabbe's like when he gets a bee in his bonnet."

"Yes, sir," said Sloan. The proper name for that was "professional opinion" but he didn't say so.

"It doesn't sound too important anyway," said Leeyes. He tore off the top sheet of a message pad and added gratuitously, "And if it's not too important you might as well take Constable Crosby with you. I can't spare anyone better today."

* * *

If she had happened to have looked out of one of the front windows of Collerton House at the right time that afternoon Elizabeth Busby might actually have seen Constable Brian Ridgeford and the Boller *père et fils* shipping the body of the dead man aboard the rowing boat. The uninterrupted view of the estuary was one of the many attractions of Collerton House. The trees planted by the first owner, which were mature now, had been carefully set back behind the building line so that the sight of the gradually broadening river was not impaired and yet the house itself was still sheltered by them.

If Elizabeth Busby had been really interested in what had been going on in the water during the afternoon she could have done more than just glance out of the window. She could have stepped out onto the stone terrace in front of the house and taken a closer look at the River Calle through the telescope that was permanently mounted there.

This telescope was currently kept trained on a pair of great crested grebes which had built their nest at the edge of a large clump of reeds, but it was so mounted that it could be swung easily from side to side and up and down to take in the entire estuary from Kinnisport and the sea to the west right up the river to Billing Bridge in the east.

The reason why Elizabeth Busby did not happen to look out of the window that afternoon was that she had so many other things to do. Collerton House had been built in more spacious times: times when servants were, if not two a penny, at least around for ten pounds a year all found. Now it was a case of first find someone willing to work at all in the house. That couldn't be done very easily any more—quite apart from the consideration of the expense.

Notwithstanding this there were very few rooms in Collerton House that did not boast a bell-push or a bell-pull of some description—some of them of a very ornate description—as a reminder of a more comfortable past. The only one of them that Elizabeth Busby knew for certain was in good working order was the one that had been in her aunt's bedroom. Aunt Celia had rung it when she was ill and Elizabeth had answered it—and had gone on answering its each and every summons right up until the day when Celia Mundill had died in that very bedroom.

Another reason why Elizabeth Busby was too busy to look out of the window was that she was deliberately undertaking as much hard work in the day as she possibly could. If there was a job that looked as if it could be packed into her waking hours then she put her hand to it and carried on until it was done. Even Frank Mundill, himself sunk in gloom since his wife's death, had advised her to let up a little.

"Take it easy, Elizabeth," he'd mumbled at breakfast time only that morning. "We don't want you cracking up as well."

"I've got to keep busy," she'd said fiercely. "Just got to! Don't you understand?"

"Sorry. Of course." He'd retreated behind the newspaper after that and said no more about it and Elizabeth Busby had gone on to devote the day to turning out the main guest room. It was too soon to be making up the bed but there was no harm in getting the room ready. Besides, giving the bedroom a thorough spring-clean somehow contrived to bring those who were going to occupy it next a little nearer.

There was some real comfort to be had in that because it was her own father and mother who were due to come to stay and who would be moving into the room. Each and every touch that she put into the spring-cleaning of the bedroom brought its own reminder of them. Quite early on she had gone off through the house in search of a bigger bedside table for her father. He always liked a decent-sized table beside his bed—not one of those tiny shelves that could take no more than book and reading glasses. He'd lived abroad for so long—usually in strange and far-away places—that he was accustomed to having everything he might need in the night right beside him.

She'd never forgotten his telling her that when he was a young man he used to sleep with a gun under his pillow—but she had never known whether that had been true or not. It had been the same night that she had lost a milk tooth. She had been inconsolable to start with about the tooth—or perhaps it had been about the gap that it had left.

"Put it where I put my pistol, Twiz," he'd said, "and the Tooth Fairy will find it and leave you a silver sixpence."

"Did the Tooth Fairy find your pistol?" she had wanted to know, forgetting all about her tooth. "What did she leave you for your pistol?"

That had been on one of her parents' rare and glorious leaves when for once they had all been together as a family. Then, all too soon, it had been over and her mother and father had gone again. By the time they came back on their next furlough Elizabeth had all her second teeth and had grown out of believing in fairies of any ethereal description. Even sixpences had been practically no more.

So today she'd humped an occasional table along to the guest bedroom to put beside the bed. She even knew which side of the bed her father would choose to sleep on. The side nearer the door. That was another legacy from years of living in foreign and sometimes dangerous places . . .

The table had been heavier than she had expected but when she came to move it she realised that Frank Mundill must have gone back to work—his office was in the converted studio right at the top of the house—and so wasn't around to give her a hand. That was after they'd had a scratch luncheon together in the kitchen—Mundill had heated up some soup and rummaged about in the refrigerator until he'd found a wedge of pâté for them both. He'd hovered over the electric toaster for a while and promised to rustle up something more substantial that evening.

"Don't worry, Frank." She'd brushed her hair back from her face as she spoke. "I'm not hungry."

"Can't honestly say that I am either," he shrugged wryly. "Still, we'd better try to eat something, I suppose . . ."

She had given him a look of genuine pity. Frank Mundill's profession might be architect but his great hobby was cooking and it had been quite pathetic during his wife's last illness to see him trying to tempt her failing appetite with special delicacy after special delicacy. On her part Celia Mundill had gallantly tried to swallow a mouthful or so of each as long as she had the strength to do so—but the time had come when even that was more than she could manage.

"I'll have the bedroom done by tonight," Elizabeth had said abruptly. She tried not to think about Aunt Celia's last illness. It was too soon for that.

"Don't overdo it, though, will you, Elizabeth?"

She shook her head.

Only her father and mother were allowed to call her Twiz. With everyone else she insisted upon Elizabeth in full. None of the other traditional diminutives were permitted either. She never answered to Liz or Betty or Beth or—save the mark—Bess. Peter had teased her about that once.

"Even Queen Elizabeth didn't mind that," he'd said. "Good Queen Bess rolls around the tongue rather nicely, don't you think?"

"No, I don't, and don't you dare call me Bess either, Peter Hinton. I won't have it!"

And now she had to try not to think about Peter Hinton either.

"Give me a call when you're ready for some tea," she'd said to Frank Mundill that afternoon. His secretary was on holiday this week. "I expect I'll still be up in the bedroom," she added. "I'm making a proper job of it while I'm about it."

So the afternoon—the afternoon that the body of the unknown man was brought ashore at Edsway—passed for her in hard work. It was the only way in which Elizabeth Busby could get through the days. Anyway it wasn't so much the days—they were just periods of time to be endured—as the nights. It was the nights that were the greatest burden.

They were pure hell.

For the first time in her life Elizabeth had come to see the long stretches of the night as something to be feared. The leaden march of the night hours shook her soul in a way that the hours of the day didn't. The days were easier. There were punctuations in the day. There were, too, the constant demands of civilised behaviour to be met and there were the recurring needs of her body to be attended to. She had to wash, to dress, to eat and to drink—even if she could no longer be merry. All the blessedness of a routine was there for the using.

She found rather to her surprise that she washed, dressed and—sometimes—ate just as she had always done. She answered the telephone, wrote letters, did the dusting and attended—acolyte-fashion—to the washing machine just as if nothing had happened.

That was in the daytime.

It was a constant source of wonder to her that after the day when her own heaven had fallen and "The hour when earth's foundations fled" she still got through the days at all.

The nights, of course, were different.

In a world that had tumbled about her ears the nights had turned into refined torture. There was no routine about the long watches of the night, no demands on her time to be met until morning, and no requirement of her body that could be satisfied—not even sleep.

Especially not sleep.

The nighttime was when she could have walked mile after mile—however weary she had been when she dropped into bed. Instead custom required that she spend it lying still in a narrow bed in a small room. The room—her room—got smaller and smaller during the night. She could swear to it. There had been a horror story she'd read once when she was young about the roof of a four-poster bed descending on the person in the bed and smothering him . . .

She'd been of an age to take horror in her stride then, to laugh at it even. Horror in those days had been something weird and strange. Now she was older she knew that horror was merely something familiar gone sadly wrong . . . that was where true horror lay . . .

Why, she thought angrily to herself as she shook out a duster, hadn't someone like Wilkie Collins written about the bruising a girl's soul suffered when she'd been jilted? That should have given any novelist worth his salt something to get his teeth into . . .

CHAPTER 3

Tell the Sheriff's Officers that I am ready.

Detective Constable Crosby—he who could most easily be spared from the police station—brought the car round for Detective Inspector Sloan as that officer stepped out of the back door of Berebury Police Station.

The constable was patently disappointed to learn that there was no hurry to get to wherever they were going.

"No hurry at all," repeated Sloan, climbing into the front passenger seat. "You can take it from me, Crosby, that this particular problem isn't going to run away."

The other man withdrew his hand from the switches to the blue flashing light and siren.

"On the contrary," forecast Detective Inspector Sloan, "I shouldn't be surprised if it's not going to be with us for quite a while."

The trouble with Superintendent Leeyes was that his gloom was catching.

"Yes, sir," said Crosby, immediately losing interest. "Where to, then, slowly?"

And the trouble with Detective Constable Crosby was that he was only nearly insubordinate.

Sloan settled himself in the car, reminding himself of something he knew very well already: that Detective Constable Crosby wasn't by any means the brightest star in the Force's firmament. As far as he, Sloan, could make out, the only thing that Crosby really liked doing was driving fast cars fast. That was probably why Inspector Harpe, who was in charge of

Traffic Division, had insisted that the constable was better in the plain clothes branch rather than the uniform one.

"Call us 'Woollies' if you like, Sloan," Harpe had said vehemently at the time.

"I don't . . ." began Sloan; though there were those in plenty who did.

"But," swept on Inspector Harpe, "I'm not stupid enough to want that boy Crosby behind the wheel of one of Traffic Division's vehicles."

"No, Harry."

"First time he was tempted," sniffed Harpe, "he'd be after a ton-up kid."

For Adam and Eve temptation had been an apple.

For a traffic duty policeman temptation was a youth behind the wheel of a fast car ahead of him and going faster, ever faster. The driver would be showing the world in general—but the police car in particular—what his car would do. If it was his car: ten to one it would be somebody else's car. Taken for a joy ride. Taken on a joy ride, too.

Luring on the Law was practically a parlour game.

And as Inspector Harpe of Traffic Division knew only too well, what was begun "sae rantingly, sae wantonly, sae dauntingly" usually ended up on Robert Burns's present-day equivalent of the gallows-tree—a fatal motorway pile-up. Because, as a rule, the Law's cars could do rather better than anyone else's, and the Law's drivers were trained. They were trained, too, of course, not to respond to taunting behaviour. That training, though, took a little longer than learning to drive well.

"The first time someone tried it on Crosby," Harpe had predicted, "he'd fall for it. You know he would, Sloan. Be honest now."

"Well . . ."

"Hook, line and sinker, I'll be bound," said Harpe. "I'm prepared to bet good money that he'd go and chase some madman right up the motorway until they ran out of road. Both of them."

"But . . ." Even Superintendent Leeyes wasn't usually as bodeful as this.

"Catch Crosby radioing ahead to get the tearaway stopped instead of going after him."

"Oh, come off it, Harry," Sloan had said at the time. "You were young once yourself."

At this moment now he contented himself with telling Crosby where to go. "Dr. Dabbe is expecting us at the mortuary," he said as the police car swung round Berebury's new multi-storey car park and out onto the main road.

Crosby automatically put his foot down.

"In due course," said Sloan swiftly. "Not on two stretchers."

The consultant pathologist to the Berebury District Hospital Group was more than expecting them. He was obviously looking forward to seeing the two policemen. He welcomed them both to his domain. "Come along in, Inspector Sloan, and—let me see now—it's Constable Crosby, isn't it?"

"Yes, Doctor." Crosby didn't like attending post-mortem examinations.

The pathologist was rubbing his hands together. "We've got something very interesting here, gentlemen. Very interesting indeed."

"Have we?" said Sloan warily. Cases that were "open and shut" were what made for a quiet life, not interesting ones.

The pathologist indicated the door to the post-mortem theatre. "What you might call a real puzzler."

"Really?" said Sloan discouragingly.

"As well as being 'a demd, damp, moist, unpleasant body' as Mr. Mantalini said."

"Not drowned, anyway, I hear," advanced Sloan, who did not know who Mr. Mantalini was. The case was never going to get off the ground at all at this rate.

"Not 'drowned dead' anyway," agreed the pathologist breezily. "You know your Charles Dickens, I expect, Sloan?"

Sloan didn't but that wasn't important. What was important was what the pathologist had found.

He waited.

"In my opinion," said Dr. Dabbe, getting to the point at last, "confirmed, I may say, by some X-ray photographs, this chap we've got here . . . whoever he is . . ."

"Yes?" said Sloan, stifling any other comment. The body's identity was something else that the police were going to have to establish.

Later.

". . . and however wet he is," continued the pathologist imperturbably, "was dead before he hit the water."

"Ah," said Sloan.

"Furthermore . . ."

Even Constable Crosby raised his head at this.

"Furthermore," said the pathologist, "in my opinion he died from the consequences of a fall from a considerable height."

Detective Constable Crosby clearly felt it was incumbent on him to say something into the silence which followed this pronouncement. He looked round the room and said, "Did he fall or was he pushed?"

"Ah, gentlemen," Dr. Dabbe said courteously, "I rather think that your department, isn't it? Not mine."

Detective Inspector Sloan was not to be diverted by such pleasantry. There were still some matters that were the pathologist's department and he wanted to know about them.

"What sort of height?" he asked immediately.

"Difficult to say exactly at this stage, Sloan," temporised the pathologist. "There's a lot of work to be done yet. I've got to take a proper look at the X-rays, too. I can tell you that there are multiple impacted fractures where the shock effect of hitting *terra firma* ran through the body."

Sloan winced involuntarily.

The pathologist was more detached. "It demonstrates Newton's Third Law of Motion very nicely—you know, the one about force travelling through a body."

Sloan didn't know and didn't care.

"He didn't fall from the air, did he?" he asked. There had been parts of a dead body dropped from an aeroplane on the Essex marshes just after the last war. That case had become a *cause célèbre* and passed into legal history and he, Sloan, had read about it. "We're not talking about aeroplane height, are we?"

"No, no," said Dr. Dabbe. "Less than that."

Sloan nodded. "But he didn't fall into the water?"

"Not first," said the pathologist. "I think he hit the earth first."

That only left fire. If Sloan had been a medieval man he would have promptly enquired about the fourth element—fire—that always went with earth, water and air. He wasn't, he reminded himself astringently, any such thing. He was a twentieth-century policeman. "A fall from a height," he said sedately instead.

"Yes," said the pathologist.

"And onto hard ground," said Sloan.

"Hard something," said Dr. Dabbe. "As to whether it was ground or not I can't say yet."

"Not into the sea, though?" concluded Sloan.

That stirred Detective Constable Crosby into speech again. "What about Cranberry Point?" he suggested. "That's a good drop."

"Rather less than that, too, I think," said Dr. Dabbe more slowly, "though I can't tell you for certain yet. I'll have to have a look at the exact degree of bone displacement . . ."

The knee bone was connected to the hip bone and the hip bone was connected to the thigh bone . . .

"You can get out onto the cliff above Kinnisport," persisted Crosby, "if you have a mind to."

"But," pointed out the pathologist, "if you go over the cliff there you don't hit the water."

"No more you don't, Doctor," agreed the constable, in no whit put out.

Sloan had forgotten for a moment that the pathologist was a Sunday sailor himself. He remembered now that Dr. Dabbe sailed an Albacore somewhere in the estuary. He was bound to know that stretch of the river and coastline well.

"You hit the rocks if you go over the edge up there," pronounced Dr. Dabbe, thus revealing that he had already given the cliffs beyond Kinnisport some thought.

"But not the water," agreed Sloan. That was what had saved Cranberry Point from becoming Calleshire's Beachy Head all right. "The tide never comes in to the very bottom of the cliff."

"Exactly," said Dr. Dabbe. "He wouldn't have ended up in the water if he'd gone over the cliffs there."

"Unless," said Inspector Sloan meticulously, "someone had then punted the body into the sea." It might be Dr. Dabbe's function to establish the cause of death; it was Detective Inspector Sloan's bounden duty to consider all the angles of a proposition. "After he'd fallen . . ."

"Or been pushed," said Crosby unnecessarily.

It was Sloan whom the pathologist answered. "Yes, Inspector, I suppose you shouldn't discount the theoretical possibility that someone dragged him off the rocks at the foot of the cliff and into the sea."

"They'd have had a job," said Crosby roundly, forgetting that it was no part of the office of constable—detective or otherwise—to argue with an inspector—detective or otherwise—let alone with a full-blown medical man.

Sloan regarded Crosby with a certain curiosity. It wasn't the breach of protocol that intrigued him. After all, protocol was only significant in one of two ways—either in its observance or in its breaching. What he had noted was that Detective Constable Crosby—traffic policeman *manqué*—didn't as a rule take such an interest in a case early on. He wondered what it was about the matter so far that had caught his wayward attention.

"I must say, Sloan," added Dr. Dabbe, who never minded with whom he argued, "from my own experience I can confirm that it would be the devil's own job to get in there under the cliffs with a boat to do any such thing."

"Would it, Doctor?" Cranberry Point, then, could be discounted.

"It certainly wouldn't be a job for a man on his own," said Dabbe, "and the tide would have had to be exactly right."

"And as for walking round the cliffs from Kinnisport, sir," put in Crosby.

"Yes?" said Sloan, interested in spite of himself. Crosby was no walker. His stint on the beat had proved that.

"You'd have your work cut out to do it, sir, without the coastguards seeing you."

If Superintendent Leeyes had been there he would have automatically added a rider to the effect that the coastguards hadn't anything else to do but look out at the sea and the cliffs. The superintendent wasn't there, of course, because he never went out on cases at all if he could help it. He stayed at the centre while his myrmidons fanned out and then reported back. The still centre, some might say; others were more perceptive and spoke wisely of the eye of the hurricane . . .

"Exactly," said Dr. Dabbe, who was fortunately able to concentrate entirely on the matter in hand. Forensic pathologists didn't have superior officers chasing them. In theory, at any rate, they pursued absolute accuracy for its own sake—at the request of Her Majesty's Coroner and at the behest of no one else. The only people of whom pathologists had to be wary, thought Sloan with a certain amount of envy, were opposing counsel in court who wanted to give the Goddess of Truth a tweak here and there to the benefit of their particular client.

Detective Inspector Sloan took out of his notebook the copy that he had brought with him of Constable Ridgeford's brief report. "Our man at Edsway says that there weren't any clues as to this chap's name at all that he could see."

"And none that we could either," agreed the pathologist. "Not to his name," he added obscurely. "We'll have to leave his personal identity to you people, Sloan, for the time being. Even his own mother wouldn't know him now."

Sloan nodded. The doctor's "we" included his own assistant, Burns, a taciturn man who rarely spoke, but who would have gone through the dead man's clothes with the meticulousness of an old-fashioned nanny. "We'll need as much as we can to go on, Doctor."

The pathologist started to take his jacket off and to look about him for a green gown. "His physical identity's no problem."

"Good," said Sloan warmly.

"He's male," said Dr. Dabbe, obligingly beginning at the very beginning.

Sloan wrote that down. The Genesis touch, you could say. "And how old, Doctor?"

Surely that did come after sex, didn't it?

"About twenty-three," said the doctor promptly. "Give or take a year or two either way."

Sloan looked down at his notebook and wondered what came next in the pathologist's logical sequence after sex and age.

"As to his race . . ." began Dr. Dabbe cautiously.

"Yes?" Perhaps a seaman from an alien country had found landfall on an English shore after all . . .

"Caucasian," said Dabbe, reaching for his surgical gown.

Detective Constable Crosby jerked his head dismissively. "Oh, he's a foreigner then, is he?"

"Not necessarily, Constable." The doctor grinned. "We're all Caucasians here, you know." He waved a hand at his assistant, Burns, who had just entered the office. "Even Burns, here, and he's a Scotsman."

"Ready when you are, Doctor," said Burns impassively.

The pathologist led the way through to the post-mortem room.

CHAPTER 4

To die a dry death at land,
Is as bad as a watery grave.

Horace Boller had never been a man to let the grass grow under his feet. Nor was he one to share confidences—not even with his own son. Certainly not with Mrs. Boller. After he had got back from Edsway with the body of the unknown man he saw it off in his cousin Ted's hearse and then stumped along to his own cottage where he proceeded to sink a vast mug of steaming hot tea at speed.

"That's better," he said, wiping his mouth with the back of his hand. Almost immediately he got up to go out again, pushing his chair back as he did so. It scraped on the floor.

Had he known it, the dialogue he then embarked upon with his wife strongly resembled that between many a parent and an adolescent child.

"Where are you going then, Horace?" she asked, casting an eye in the direction of a saucepan on the cooking stove.

"Out," he rasped.

"Where?"

"Nowhere."

"When will you be back?"

"Don't know."

Horace was nearer sixty than sixteen but saw no more need to amplify what he said than did a rebellious teenager. Mrs. Boller sniffed and turned down the flame under the saucepan.

"You'll have to wait for your supper then."

From the cottage doorway all he said was, "Expect me when you see me."

And that was said roughly. His mind was on something else.

If that was too soon for Mrs. Boller she did not say.

There were some homes that were entirely maintained on the well-established premise that the husband and father was "a saint abroad and a devil at home"; or it may have been that Mrs. Boller had just given up the unequal struggle.

Horace, on the other hand, hadn't given up anything and was soon back at the shore pushing his rowing boat out again. The agglomeration of buoys, hardstanding and wooden rafts was too informal to be dignified with the name of marina but that was its function. Horace poked about this way and that, and then, calculating that anyone watching his movements from the village would by now have lost interest in his activities, he steered his prow in a seaward direction and bent his back to the oars.

He was as subconsciously aware of the state of the tide as a farmer was aware of the weather and a motorist of other vehicles on the road. With a nicely judged spurt of effort he moved with the last of the tide before he turned distinctly up river and into fresh water. After a little time in the middle of the stream he let the boat drift inshore again towards the south shore—the same side of the river as Edsway but farther up river.

It was a compound of long experience and the river lore of generations that kept Horace Boller from grounding his boat on the mud banks. He seemed to know by instinct how to pick his way up river and which channel had deep water in it, and which only looked as if it had. It wasn't only the apparent depths of the channels that were deceptive. Some of those which looked the most promising led only to the shallows. Horace Boller, however, seemed also to know where each one went. Daedalus-like, he selected one channel and passed by another with the sureness of much practice.

Presently he found himself in relatively deep water in spite of being near the shore. This was where the river cut alongside the edge of the parish of Collerton. The churchyard came right down to the river bank and as it had got more and more full over the years the land towards the river side had been used for graves.

It was undoubtedly picturesque and in the summertime holidaymakers would come to stroll along the bank and through the churchyard exclaiming at the fine views of the estuary to be had from the little promontory. They seldom came in the winter and never in the spring and autumn when the grand alliance of wind and water almost always flooded the whole bank and part of the churchyard.

The land was dry now and from where he was in his boat Horace could see someone tending one of the graves near the river. He bent to his oars though and carried on upstream without looking up. Presently he passed Collerton House too. Like the churchyard, its land—in this case, lawn—came down to the river's edge. There was a little landing stage by the water and beyond that a small boathouse. After that there were no more dwellings, only open fields. The main street of Collerton was set back from the church. Those who professed to understand the English rural landscape were in the habit of speaking knowledgeably about the devastation of the Black Death.

"That's when all the little hovels round the church decayed," they would say, "and a later medieval village grew up some distance away from the old diseased houses."

Horace Boller, who said, "It stands to reason" almost as often as the storybook character Worzel Gummidge, knew perfectly well why the church stood in lonely splendour apart from the village. It had been built on the only patch of remotely high ground in the parish. The houses had been built well back from the river's edge for the elementary—and elemental—reason that the other land was liable to flooding. Horace was a fisherman. He knew all about the elements.

He rowed steadily up river for purposes of his own. He didn't stop in his progress until he rounded the last bend before Billing Bridge. Only then did he turn his craft and allow the current to help carry him along and back to the estuary and Edsway. On his way home he looked in on Ted Boller, back in his carpenter's shed after his trip to Berebury. When he got back indoors his wife asked him where he'd been.

"Nowhere," he said.

"Did you see anyone?"

"No one better than myself," he said obscurely.

"What have you been doing then?"

"Nothing."

All of which was—in its own way—perfectly true.

* * *

Detective Inspector Sloan entered the mortuary and took his first reluctant look at the unknown male of Caucasian stock, aged about twenty-three years. A decomposing body was not a pretty sight.

"He's not undernourished," said Dr. Dabbe, who had led the way.

Burns, his assistant, who had brought up the rear, said, "I've got a note of his exact weight and height for you, Doctor."

Deadweight, thought Sloan to himself, was a word they used about ships, too. He took a look at the man for himself, automatically noting that there was nothing about him to show that he had been a seaman.

"He's not overweight either, Doctor," he said aloud. That was something to be noted, too, these days. Would historians of the future call this the Age of Corpulence?

"Average," agreed Dr. Dabbe. "Dark hair and brown eyes . . . are you making a note of that, Constable?"

"Short back and sides," observed Sloan. That, in essence, would tell Superintendent Leeyes what he wanted to know. For the superintendent the length of a man's hair divided the sheep from the goats as neatly as that chap in the Bible had sorted out the men whom he wanted in his army by the way in which they had drunk at the edge of the water. He'd forgotten his name . . .

"Short back and sides," agreed the pathologist. "What's left of it."

Gideon, thought Sloan to himself: that's who it was. He'd beaten the army of the Midianites with his hand-picked men, had Gideon.

"I've been looking for occupational signs for you," said Dr. Dabbe.

"That would help," said Sloan warmly. "In fact, Doctor, anything would help at this stage. Anything at all."

"You haven't got anyone like him on the books as missing, then," said the doctor, correctly interpreting this.

"Not in Calleshire," said Sloan. "Not male."

Detective Constable Crosby hitched a shoulder in his corner. "Plenty of girls missing, Doctor. All looking older than they are. All good home-loving girls," he added, "except that they've left home."

The white slave trade mightn't be what it had been but it kept going. It wasn't, however, Sloan's immediate concern. He kept his mind on the matter in hand: an unknown body. "What sort of occupational signs, Doctor?"

"Well, he's quite muscular, Sloan. You can see that for yourself. I'd say he wasn't a man used to sitting at a desk all day. Or if he was, he went in for some strenuous sport too."

Sloan wondered what the masculine equivalent of housemaid's knee was.

"Actually," said Dabbe, "there's no specific sign of a trade about him at all."

"Ah," said Sloan non-committally.

"He didn't have cobbler's knee or miller's thumb," said the pathologist, "and I can't find any other mark on his person that's come from using the same tool day after day."

Sloan wondered what sort of occupational mark the police force made on a man—day after day. Varicose veins, probably.

"And he isn't covered in oil," said Dr. Dabbe.

Oil wouldn't have come off in the water, Sloan knew that.

As a possible cause of death shipwreck after a fall on board receded a little from the front of his mind.

"There's something else that isn't there," said the pathologist.

"What's that, Doctor?" All that came into Sloan's mind was that ridiculous verse of everyone's childhood: "I met a man who wasn't there . . ."

"Nicotine stains," replied Dr. Dabbe prosaically. "I should say he was a non-smoker."

"We don't know at this stage what will be a help."

"Well, I hope you aren't counting on a fingerprint identification because this chap's skin's more than a bit bloated over now."

Even the deceased's physical identity was taking a little time to put together.

"Fingernails—what's left of them—appear to have been clean and well cared for," continued Dabbe.

"Make a note of that, Crosby," commanded Sloan. Manners might maketh man but appearance mattered too.

"As far as I can see," said the pathologist, "he was clean generally."

That, too, ruled out a whole subculture of the voluntarily dirty. The involuntarily dirty didn't have well-cared-for fingernails and they weren't well nourished as a rule either.

"And he's not a horny-handed son of the soil," concluded Sloan aloud. "Is that all you can tell us, Doctor, from the—er—outside, so to speak?"

"Bless you, no, Sloan," said the pathologist cheerfully. "That's only half of my superficial examination. I, of course, use the word 'superficial' in its purely anatomical connotation of appertaining to the surface, not in its pejorative one."

"Naturally," murmured Sloan pacifically. The doctor wasn't in court now. He didn't have to choose his words so carefully.

"And for the record," added the pathologist breezily, "he hasn't any distinguishing marks within the meaning of the Act."

Detective Inspector Sloan nodded, any vision he might have had of easy identification fading away. Even with what the Passport Office engagingly called "special peculiarities" listed just for that very reason—to help identify a particular person—it wasn't always easy. Without them it could be very difficult indeed. "Anything else, Doctor?"

"He wasn't mainlining on drugs . . ."

Times had certainly changed. Once upon a time drug-taking

hadn't been one of the characteristics of dead young men that pathologists looked for and—having found them—echoed Housman's parodist, "What, still alive at twenty-two . . . ?"

"There are no signs of repeated injections anywhere," said Dr. Dabbe smoothly, "and no suspicious 'spider's web' tattoos on the inside of the forearm to cover up those signs."

An old art put to a new use.

"No tattooing at all, in fact," said Dr. Dabbe, proceeding in an orderly manner through the fruits of his superficial examination.

Detective Constable Crosby made a note of that.

"His ears haven't been pierced either," remarked the pathologist.

Times had certainly changed. Detective Inspector Sloan decided that he was getting old. Unpierced ears were a feature that he should have noticed for himself. The Long John Silver touch was something that had grown up since he was a boy. When he, Sloan, saw ear-rings on a man he was still old-fashioned enough to look beyond them for the wooden leg.

"In fact, Doctor," concluded Sloan aloud, "he was a pretty ordinary sort of man."

"You want to call him John Citizen, do you?" Dr. Dabbe raised a quizzical eyebrow. "There you would be barking up the wrong tree, Sloan."

"He seems ordinary enough to me," persisted Sloan.

"There's no such thing as an ordinary man," responded Dr. Dabbe instantly. "We're all quite different, Sloan. That's the beauty of the system."

"There doesn't appear," he said flatly, "to be anything out of the ordinary about this man." One thing that Sloan wasn't going to do was to get into that sort of debate with the pathologist.

"Ah, but I'm not finished yet, Sloan."

Dr. Dabbe had in some respects hardly started. He beckoned Sloan nearer to the post-mortem table and tilted an inspection lamp slightly. "You will observe, Sloan, that this man—whoever he is—has been in the water for quite a time."

Sloan repressed a slight shudder. "Yes, Doctor."

"And," continued the pathologist, "that in spite of this the body is scarcely damaged."

Detective Inspector Sloan obediently leaned forward and peered at the supine figure.

"The lack of damage is interesting," declared Dr. Dabbe.

Sloan held his peace. If the pathologist wanted to be as oracular as Sherlock Holmes and start talking about dogs not barking in the night there was very little that he, Sloan, could do about it.

"It isn't consistent with the length of time the body has been in the water, Sloan."

So that was what was interesting the doctor . . .

Before Sloan could speak the pathologist had moved the shadowless overhead lamp yet again. This time the beam was thrown over the deceased's left hand.

"There are a couple of grazes on what's left of the skin of the fingers," he remarked in a detached way. "He might—only might, mind you, Sloan—have got them trying to save himself from falling."

Sloan tightened his lips. For all his scientific objectivity, it wasn't a nice picture that the pathologist had just conjured up.

CHAPTER 5

For death is a debt,
A debt on demand.

Although Horace Boller had told his wife that he had seen nothing and nobody and had been nowhere he had, in fact, noticed that there had been someone in Collerton churchyard when he had rowed upstream past it. Whoever it was who was there had looked up as he drew level with the churchyard in his rowing boat but Horace hadn't paused in his steady pulling at the oars as he went by. It didn't do to pause if you were rowing against the current. Coming downstream was different. You could even ship oars coming down on the current if you caught the river in the right place.

So Horace, although never averse to a little bit of a gossip with anyone—he collected sundry information in the same way that some men collected postage stamps—had pulled away at the oars and passed by without speaking. He hadn't gone on his way, though, without recognising the figure tending the grave by the river. Most people who lived round about the shores of the estuary knew Mr. Mundill's wife's niece, Elizabeth Busby, by sight. She'd been coming to Collerton House on and off for her school holidays ever since she was a little girl. She'd practically grown up by the river, in fact, and when her aunt, Mrs. Celia Mundill, had fallen ill, it had seemed only right that she should give up her job and come back to Collerton to nurse her. Had been engaged to be married, too, Horace had heard, but not any longer.

By the time Horace Boller came down river on his return

journey she had gone from the churchyard and all he could see from the river was a fine display of pale pink roses on the new grave.

Elizabeth Busby hadn't planned to visit the Collerton graveyard that afternoon at all. She had fully intended to finish spring-cleaning the guest room and leave it all ready and waiting for the day—the welcome day—when her parents would arrive from South America. What had made her change her mind about finishing preparing the room was something so silly that she didn't even like to think about it. She'd swept and dusted the room and moved the furniture about and taken the curtains down before she even noticed that the picture over the bed had been changed.

She had stopped the vacuum cleaner in full flight so to speak and had stood stock still in the middle of the floor, staring.

There was no shortage of pictures in Collerton House. On the contrary, it had them everywhere. But everywhere. Her grandfather, Richard Camming, had been an enthusiastic amateur artist and his efforts were hanging in every room of the house. He was not exactly an original . . . The painting that had hung over the bed in the guest room ever since she could remember had been a water-colour of a composition owing a great deal to the works of the late Richard Parkes Bonington.

It had been replaced by an oil painting done in what his two daughters—her aunt Celia and her own mother—affectionately called their father's "Burne-Jones period." Richard Camming had even called it "Ophelia" and Elizabeth knew it well. The portrayal of Ophelia's drowning in a stream usually lived on the upstairs landing not far from the top of the stairs.

"He might have put it nearer the bathroom," her own father used to say irreverently. "All that water going to waste . . ."

Elizabeth Busby had rested her hands on the vacuum cleaner in the same way as a gardener rested his on his spade while she considered this.

She was not in any doubt about the pictures having been changed; she knew them both too well. And if she had been in two minds about it a thin line of unfaded wallpaper under the new picture—hidden a little from the casual gaze by the frame

—would have confirmed it. The size of the new picture didn't exactly match that of the old.

As soon as she had taken in this evidence—before her very eyes, as the conjurers said—she had gone out onto the landing to look there for the painting that usually hung over the head of the spare bedroom bed. It had been of a stretch of beach . . . When she got to the top of the stairs, though, to the spot where Grandfather's version of Ophelia usually hung the painting of the beach—presumably at Edsway (after Bonington)—wasn't there in its stead.

There wasn't a gap there either of course.

Elizabeth would have noticed a gap straightaway. Everyone would have noticed a gap. What was there in the place of Ophelia drowning among the lilies—it must have been a very slow-moving stream, she thought inconsequentially—was a water-colour of the estuary of the River Calle as seen from Collerton House. This owed nothing to any artist save Richard Camming himself and it was not very good. Moreover it was a view that he had painted many, many times—like Monet and the River Thames.

"And not got any better at it," decided Elizabeth judiciously.

Unlike Monet.

There were at least a dozen efforts by Richard Camming at capturing on canvas the oxbow of the river as it swept down towards the sea at Collerton. This particular painting could have been any one of them. Elizabeth wasn't aware of having seen this one anywhere else in the house before but there were several piles of pictures stacked away in the attics of Collerton House and it could easily have been among them without her knowing.

She went back at once to the bedroom to check that only one picture had been changed. Over the fireplace there had hung throughout her lifetime a picture in which her grandfather had tried to capture the elusive gregariousness of the work of Sir David Wilkie—the Scottish Breughel. Richard Camming hadn't actually got a blind fiddler in the picture but there was a general feeling that the musician wasn't far away.

That picture was still there. Elizabeth was not surprised. She would have noticed much earlier in the day if there had been any change in the picture hanging over the fireplace. The head of the bed, though, was at an angle from the window and only got full sunshine in the afternoon.

She had tried after this to go back to her vacuum cleaning but her determined concentration on the mundane had been broken and suddenly her thoughts and carefully suppressed emotions were unleashed in unruly turmoil.

Abruptly she left the cleaner where it was standing in the middle of the floor and went out of the bedroom. As she looked over the landing balustrade she saw with approval the glass case reposing on a window sill in the entrance hall. There was absolutely nothing amateur about her great-grandfather's legacy to posterity. What he had left behind him had been something much more useful than dozens and dozens of indifferent paintings. Gordon Camming—Richard Camming's father—had designed a valve that the marine engineering world of his day had fallen upon with delight and used ever since.

A Camming valve had been fitted into a model and stood for all the world to see in the house built by its designer with the proceeds of the patent. But it was really paintings and not patents that Elizabeth Busby had on her mind as she passed along the landing on her way to Frank Mundill's office. The studio, with its mandatory north light added fifty years earlier by an indulgent father for his painter son, served now as the drawing office of Frank Mundill, architect. Elizabeth didn't usually disturb him there, although she'd done so once or twice when her aunt had taken a turn for the worse—not otherwise —but she didn't hesitate now.

And almost immediately she wished that she hadn't.

Another time she would make a point of not going to his office unheralded because Frank Mundill was not alone. Sitting in the client's chair in his room was a neighbour—Mrs. Veronica Feckler.

"Elizabeth, my dear," said Mrs. Feckler at once, "how nice to see you."

"I'm sorry," said Elizabeth gruffly. "I didn't know there was anyone here."

"How could you?" asked Veronica Feckler blandly. "I crept round the back with my miserable little plans. I was sure that Frank was going to laugh at them and he did."

"I certainly did not," protested Frank Mundill.

"I'm sure I detected a twitch of the lips," insisted Mrs. Feckler. She was a widow who had come to live in the village of Collerton about three years ago. Elizabeth's aunt had not greatly cared for her.

"It's just," said the architect with professional caution, "that it's a long way from a quick sketch on the back of an envelope . . ."

"A shopping list, actually," murmured Mrs. Feckler.

". . . to the finished design that a builder can use."

She turned to Elizabeth. "I had this brilliant idea while I was in the greengrocer's," she said eagerly. "Dear old Mr. Partridge was telling me about Costa Rican bananas—did you know that they grew bananas in Costa Rica?"

Elizabeth knew a great deal about Costa Rica, but Mrs. Feckler hadn't waited for an answer.

"I said I'd have three when I suddenly thought what about building out over my kitchen."

"I see," said Elizabeth politely.

"And it's an even bigger step from the plans to the finished building," warned Frank Mundill. "Clients don't always realise that either."

"But I do." She turned protestingly to Elizabeth. "Tell him I do, there's a darling."

"I was turning out a bedroom," said Elizabeth obliquely, conscious that she must look more than a little scruffy. Mrs. Feckler was wearing clothes so casual that they must have needed quite a lot of time to assemble.

"And I was wasting your poor uncle's time," said the other woman, sensitive to something in Elizabeth's manner. She rose to go. "But I do really want something doing to my little cottage now that Simon has said he's coming back home for a while." She gave a little light laugh. "Mothers do have their uses sometimes."

Elizabeth assented politely to this, silently endorsing the sentiment. She would be so thankful to see her own mother again. Mrs. Busby hadn't come back to England from South America for her sister's funeral because she couldn't travel by air. Pressurised air travel didn't suit a middle-aged woman suffering from Ménière's disease of the middle ear. Even now, though, both her parents were on the high seas on their way home from South America. They had been coming for a wedding . . .

Frank Mundill was still studying the piece of paper that Mrs. Feckler had given him. "I'll have to think about this, Veronica, when I've had a chance to look at it properly."

He was rewarded with a graceful smile.

"Give me a day or so," he said hastily, "and then come back for a chat. I'll have done a quick sketch by then."

Mrs. Veronica Feckler gathered up her handbag. "How kind . . ."

Elizabeth Busby waited until Frank Mundill returned to his drawing office after showing her out. "I came about a picture," she said.

He sank back into the chair behind his desk and ran his hands through his hair. "A picture?"

"Three pictures, actually," she said.

He looked up.

"Three pictures," she said, "that aren't where they were."

"I think I know the ones you mean," he said uneasily.

"Ophelia."

"It's been moved," he said promptly.

"I know," she said. Frank Mundill wasn't meeting her eye, though. "And a river one and a beach scene . . ."

He didn't say anything in reply.

"The beach one has gone," she said.

"I know." He was studying the blotting paper on his desk now.

"Well?"

He cleared his throat. "Peter wanted it."

"Peter?" Her voice was up at high doh before she could collect herself.

He nodded. "I knew you wouldn't like that."

"Peter Hinton?" She heard herself pronouncing his name even though she had sworn to herself again and again that her lips would never form it ever more.

Frank Mundill looked distinctly uncomfortable. "He asked me if he could have it."

"Peter Hinton asked you if he could have the picture of the beach?" she echoed on a rising note of pure disbelief. "He didn't even like pictures."

He nodded. "He asked for it, though."

"That sloppy painting?" She would have said that detective stories were more Peter's line than paintings.

"Let's say 'sentimental,'" he murmured.

"That's what I meant," she said savagely. "And you're sitting there and telling me that Peter wanted it?"

"So he said." Frank Mundill was fiddling with a protractor lying on his desk now. He gazed longingly at the drawing board over in the window.

"It wasn't something to remember me by, I hope?" All the pent-up bitterness of the last few weeks exploded in excoriating sarcasm.

"He didn't say."

"St. Bernard dogs aren't a breed that are faithful unto death, are they?" she said, starting to laugh on a high, eerie note. "If so, he should have taken the imitation Landseer."

"Not that I know of," said the architect coldly.

"That would be too funny for words," she said in tones utterly devoid of humour.

"I'm sorry if you think I shouldn't have given it to him . . ."

"Why shouldn't he have a picture?" she said wildly. "Why shouldn't he have all the pictures if he wanted them? Why shouldn't everybody have all the pictures?"

"Elizabeth, my dear girl . . ."

"Well? Why not? Answer me that!"

"If you remember," Frank Mundill said stiffly, "I wasn't

aware of the provisions of your aunt's will at the time he asked me for it." He gave his polo-necked white sweater a little tug and said, "Strictly speaking I suppose the picture wasn't mine to give to him."

That stopped her all right.

"I didn't mean it that way, Frank," she said hastily. "You know that. That side of things isn't important." She essayed a slight smile. "Besides, there's plenty more pictures where that one came from."

"You can say that again," said Frank Mundill ruefully.

"Sorry, Frank," she said. "It's just that I'm still a bit upset . . ." Her voice trailed away in confusion. Collerton House and all its pictures—in fact the entire Camming inheritance—had come from Richard Camming equally to his two daughters—his only children—Celia Mundill and Elizabeth's mother, Marion Busby. Celia and Frank Mundill had had no children and Marion and William Busby, only one, Elizabeth.

When she had died earlier in the year Celia Mundill had left her husband, Frank, a life interest in her share of her own father's estate. At his death it was to pass to her niece, Elizabeth . . .

"There's no reason why Peter shouldn't have had a painting if he wanted one," she said, embarrassed. "It isn't even as if they're worth anything."

Mr. Hubert Cresswick of Cresswick Antiques (Calleford) Ltd. had confirmed that when he had done the valuation after her aunt's death. Very tactfully, of course. It was when he praised the frames that she'd known for certain.

"It's just," she went on awkwardly, "that I never thought that his having that particular one would be the reason why it wasn't there on the wall, like it always was."

"I should have mentioned it before," he mumbled. "Sorry."

"No reason why you should have done," she said more calmly.

What she really meant was that there were a lot of reasons why he shouldn't have done. Peter Hinton's name hadn't been mentioned in Collerton House since he'd left a note on the hall table—and with it the signet ring she'd given him. A "Keep off the grass" ring was what he'd said as he slipped it on his finger.

It didn't matter any longer, of course, what it was called. Elizabeth had returned the ring he'd given her—in the springtime, "the only pretty ring time"—the one with "I do rejoyce in thee my choyce" inscribed inside it, to Peter's lodgings in Luston.

That devotion hadn't lasted very long either.

Frank Mundill picked up the sketch Mrs. Veronica Feckler had left on his desk and appeared to give it his full attention. He said, "I suppose I'll have to go down and look at her timbers . . ."

"You will," she agreed, her mind in complete turmoil.

Elizabeth Busby hadn't known whether to laugh or to cry. On impulse she had gone out into the garden, swept up a bunch of her aunt's favourite roses—Fantin-Latour—and walked down to the churchyard by the river's edge.

She cried a little then.

CHAPTER 6

How can I support this sight!

The pathologist to the Berebury District Hospital Group was a fast worker. Nobody could complain about that. He was also a compulsive talker—out of the witness box, that is. His subjects were in no position to complain about this or, indeed, anything else. His assistant, Burns, was not able either—but for different, hierarchical, reasons—to voice any complaints about the pathologist's loquacity. Should he have been able to get a word in edgeways, that is.

In fact, Burns, worn down by listening, had retreated into a Trappist-like silence years ago. Detective Constable Crosby, normally a talker, didn't like attending post-mortems. He had somehow contrived to drift to a point in the room where, though technically present, he wasn't part of the action. It fell, therefore, to Detective Inspector Sloan to maintain some sort of dialogue with Dr. Dabbe.

"You'll be wanting to know a lot of awkward things, Sloan," said the pathologist, adjusting an overhead shadowless lamp.

"We'll settle for a few facts to begin with, Doctor," said the detective inspector equably.

"Like how long he'd been in the water, I suppose?"

"That would be useful to know."

"And damned difficult to say."

"Ah . . ."

"For sure, that is."

Sloan nodded. In this context, "for sure" meant remaining sure and certain under determined and sustained cross-examination by a hostile Queen's Counsel.

And under oath.

The pathologist ran his eyes over the body of the unknown man. "He's been there—in the water, I mean—longer than you might think, though," he said.

"I don't know that I'd thought about that at all," said Sloan truthfully.

"I have," responded Dr. Dabbe, "and I must say again that I would have expected rather more damage to the body. Something doesn't tie up."

Detective Inspector Sloan brought his gaze to bear on the post-mortem subject because it was his duty to do so but without enthusiasm. The body looked damaged enough to him. Detective Constable Crosby was concentrating his gaze on the ceiling.

"The degree of damage," pronounced the pathologist, "is not consistent with the degree of decomposition."

"We'll make a note of that," promised Sloan, pigeon-holing the information in his mind. By right, Crosby should have been regarding his notebook, not the ceiling.

"There's plenty of current in the estuary, you see, Sloan," said the doctor. "That's what makes the sailing so challenging. But current damages."

"Quite so," said Sloan, noting that fact—perhaps it was a factor, too—in his mind as well.

"To say nothing of there being a good tide," said Dr. Dabbe, "day in, day out."

"I daresay, Doctor," said Sloan diffidently, "that the tide'll still be pretty strong opposite Edsway, won't it?"

"If you'd tacked against it as often as I have," replied the pathologist grandly, "you wouldn't be asking that."

"No, Doctor, of course not." Sloan wasn't a frustrated single-handed Atlantic-crossing yachtsman himself. Growing roses was his hobby. It was one of the few relaxing pursuits that were compatible with the uncertain hours and demands of detection. Owning a sailing boat, as the doctor did, wasn't compatible with police pay either—but that was something different.

"The wind doesn't help," said Dabbe, stroking an imaginary

beard in the manner of Joshua Slocum. "You get a real funnel effect out there in mid-channel."

"I can see that you might," agreed Sloan. "What with the cliffs to the north . . ."

"And the headland above Marby to the south," completed the doctor. "That's the real villain of the piece."

Sloan was thinking about something else that wasn't going to help either and that was the official report. It would have to note that the subject was relatively undamaged but not well preserved. It was the sort of incongruity that didn't go down well with the superintendent; worse, it would undoubtedly have to be explained to him.

By Sloan.

"There's the shingle bank, too," said the doctor.

"Billy's Finger." Sloan had looked at the map. "I'm going out there presently to have a look at the lie of the land . . ."

"And the water," interjected Detective Constable Crosby.

Everyone else ignored this.

"There's always a fair bit of turbulence, too," remarked the pathologist sagely, "where the river meets the tide." It was Joshua Slocum who had sailed alone around the world but Dr. Dabbe contrived to sound every bit as experienced.

Immutable was the word that always came into Sloan's mind when people started to talk about tides. He might have been talking about tides at that moment, but it was the face of the superintendent which swam into his mental vision. He would be waiting for news.

"Let's get this straight, Doctor," he said more brusquely than he meant. "This man—whoever he is—has been in the water for a fair time."

"That is so," he agreed. "There is some evidence of adipocere being present," supplemented the pathologist, "but not to any great degree."

"But," said Sloan, "he hasn't been out where the tides and currents and fish could get hold of him for all that long?"

"That puts it very well," said Dr. Dabbe.

"And he didn't meet his death in the water?"

"I shall be conducting the customary routine test for the

widespread distribution of diatoms found in true drowning in sea or river water," said the pathologist obliquely, "but I shall be very surprised if I find any."

"Yes, Doctor," said Sloan. He wasn't absolutely sure what a diatom was—and now that the atom wasn't the indivisible building block of nature any longer he was even less sure.

Something in what the doctor had said must have caught the wayward attention of Detective Constable Crosby. He stirred and said, "You mean that that test wouldn't have done for the Brides-in-the-Bath?"

"I do," said Dr. Dabbe. "There aren't any planktons in bath water."

"And," said Sloan, gamely keeping to the business in hand, "we don't know who he is either . . ." He had just the one conviction about all things atomic—that the only really safe fast breeder was a rabbit.

"No," agreed Dabbe.

"Of course," said Sloan, "we could always try his fingerprints . . ."

"You'll be lucky," said Detective Constable Crosby, taking a quick look at what was left of the swollen and distended skin of the unknown man. He caught sight of his superior officer's face and added a belated "sir."

"We don't even know," carried on Sloan bitterly, "if he went into the river or the sea."

Unperturbed the doctor said, "I think we may be able to help you there, Sloan. Or, rather, Charley will."

"Or," continued Sloan grandly, "whether it was an accident or murder." He didn't know who Charley was.

"He didn't walk after he fell," said Dabbe. "I can tell you that for certain."

Sloan made a note. Facts were always welcome.

"And, Sloan, my man Burns has something to say to you, too." Dr. Dabbe waved an arm. "Haven't you, Burns?"

"Aye, Doctor."

"His clothes," divined Sloan quickly. "Do they tell us anything about him?"

"Mebbe, Inspector," replied Burns. "Mebbe."

"That's Gaelic for 'yes and no,'" said Dr. Dabbe.

"Well?"

Burns didn't answer and it was Dr. Dabbe who spoke. "There was something strange in one of his trouser pockets, wasn't there, Burns?"

"Yes, Doctor," said Burns.

"Something strange?" said Sloan alertly.

"Show the inspector what you found, man."

His assistant reached for a tray. Placed on it was a lump of metal almost the size and shape of a bun. It was a faded green in colour.

Detective Constable Crosby leaned over. "If that was 'lost property' we'd call it a clock pendulum."

"I'm not a metallurgist," said Dr. Dabbe, "but I should say it's solid copper."

"What is it, though?" asked Sloan, peering at it. There was a lip on one side of the bun shape.

"I can't tell you that, Sloan."

"It's not heavy enough to have been to weight him down," said Sloan, thinking aloud.

"Agreed," said Dr. Dabbe. He scratched the metal object with the edge of a surgical probe. "It's old, Sloan. And if you ask me . . ."

"Yes?"

"I should say it's been in the water a fair old time, too."

* * *

Police Constable Ridgeford of Edsway might have been green. He was also keen. He had noticed Horace Boller take out his rowing boat on the River Calle for the third time that afternoon and kept a wary but unobtrusive eye open for his return. If it had been a fishing trip that Horace Boller had been on then he had been unlucky because he had come back empty-handed for the second time that afternoon.

Brian Ridgeford did not have a boat. He didn't own a boat himself because he couldn't afford one; and as his beat did not extend out into the sea a grateful country did not feel called upon to supply him with one in the way in which it issued him with a regulation bicycle. What he did have—as his sergeant never failed to remind him—was a perfectly good pair of legs. He decided to use them to walk upstream along the river bank to Collerton.

As he remarked to his wife as he left the house, "You never know what's there until you've been to see."

"Curiosity killed the cat" was what she said to that, but then she hadn't been married very long and hadn't quite mastered the role of perfect police wife yet. She was trying hard to do so though because she added, "It's a casserole tonight, darling."

The only piece of good advice that the sergeant's wife had given her was to cook everything in a pot that could stand on the stove or in the oven without spoiling.

"Good." He kissed her and got as far as the door. "I'll be back soon," forecast Brian Ridgeford unwisely.

He, too, still had a lot to learn.

The remark wasn't exactly contrary to standing orders. It was just flying in the face of some sage advice given by one of the instructors at the Police Training School. "Never tell your wife when you're going to be back, lads," he'd said to the assembled class. "If you've told her to expect you at six o'clock, then by five minutes past six she'll be standing at the window. At ten minutes past six she'll have her worry coat on and be out in the street looking for you. By quarter past she'll have asked the woman next door what to do next and by half past six she'll be on the telephone to your sergeant." The instructor had delivered his punch line with becoming solemnity. "And the tracker dogs'll be out searching for you before you've had time to get your first pint down."

None of this potted wisdom so much as crossed Brian Ridgeford's mind as he stepped out of the police house door. He was thinking about other things. All he did do was pause in the hall where the hydrographic map of the estuary hung. He had to stoop a little to look at it properly.

It was a purely token obeisance.

Depths in metres reduced to chart datum or approximately the level of lowest astronomical tide meant very little to a landlubber like himself. He was, though, beginning to understand from sheer observation of the estuary something about drying heights. It was a form of local knowledge—almost inherited race memory, you might say—that seemed to have been born in the Boller tribe. Constable Ridgeford was having to learn it.

It was just as well that he had delayed his departure from the house for a moment or two. It meant that when the telephone bell rang a few minutes later he was not quite out of earshot. His wife came flying down the path after him—casserole forgotten.

"Brian! Brian . . . Stop!"

He halted.

"You're wanted, darling."

He turned.

"They've found a dinghy," called out Mrs. Ridgeford.

"Ah . . ."

"An empty one."

He retraced his steps in her direction.

"On the shore," she said.

"That figures." He absent-mindedly slipped an arm round her waist. "Whereabouts?"

"Over at Marby."

"Right round there?" Constable Ridgeford frowned. The tiny fishing village of Marby juxta Mare was on the coast the other side of Edsway—to the south and west. It had never been the same, local legend ran, since a Danish invasion in the ninth century.

"That's what the man said," answered Mrs. Ridgeford. "I told him you'd go straight over there. Was that right, Brian?"

Since their marriage was still at the very early stage when it was unthinkable that she could have done anything that wasn't right—the action being sanctified solely by virtue of its having been taken so to speak—this was a purely rhetorical question.

"Of course it was, darling." Brian Ridgeford nodded approvingly.

"Or," she added prettily, turning her face up towards his, "have I done the wrong thing?"

This, too, was a purely token question.

It got a purely token response in the form of a kiss.

"Where did I leave my bicycle clips?" asked Police Constable Brian Ridgeford rather breathlessly.

Marby juxta Mare was a village facing the sea. It was beyond the headland known as the Cat's Back that protected Edsway from the full rigours of the sea. The road, though, did not follow the coast. It cut across below the headland and made Marby much nearer to Edsway by land than by sea.

A man called Farebrother had taken charge of the dinghy. He was a lifeboatman and knew all about capsized dinghies.

"She wasn't upside down when we found her," he said. "And not stove in or anything like that or she'd never have reached where she did on the shore."

"Has she been there long?" asked Ridgeford cautiously. Boats, he knew, always took the feminine—like the word "victim" in the French language—but he didn't want to make a fool of himself by asking the wrong question.

"Just the length of a tide," said the lifeboatman without hesitation. "We reckon she'd have been gone again after the turn of the tide if we hadn't hauled her up a bit."

Ridgeford nodded sagely. "That's a help."

"No one'll thank you for letting a dinghy get away." Farebrother wrinkled his eyes. "It's a danger to everyone else, too, is a dinghy on the loose. No riding lights on a dinghy. You could smash into it in the dark and then where would you be?"

"Sunk," said Ridgeford.

"Depend on your size, that would," said the lifeboatman, taking this literally, "and where she hit you." He hitched his shoulder, and sniffed. "Anyways we put her where she can't do any harm and," he added, "where she can't come to any more harm either."

"Any more harm?" said Ridgeford quickly. "But I thought you said she wasn't damaged . . ."

"So I did," said Farebrother. "But she must have come to some harm to be out on the loose like she was, mustn't she? That's not right."

"I see what you mean," said the constable. Put lost dinghies into the same category in your mind as lost children and things fell into place.

"An insecure mooring is the least that can have happened." Farebrother picked up his oilskin jacket. He was a tall man with a thin, elongated face and high cheek-bones. From his appearance he might have descended directly from marauding Viking stock.

"I don't think that that's what it was," said the young policeman, mindful of the dead body that he'd helped to bring ashore that afternoon.

"Anyways," said the other man, "she's safe enough now. She's over this way . . . the other side of the lifeboat station . . . just follow me."

This was easier said than done. Farebrother set off at a cracking pace along the rocky sea-shore of Marby juxta Mare, so different from the fine estuary sands of Edsway, his seaboots crunching on the stones. Constable Ridgeford stepped more cautiously after him, slipping and sliding as he tried to pick his way over the difficult terrain. Farebrother slackened his pace only once. That was when a small trawler suddenly emerged from the harbour mouth. He stopped and took a good look at it. Ridgeford stopped too.

"Something wrong?" he asked.

"She's cutting it a bit fine, that's all."

"Cutting what?" asked Ridgeford. He could read the name *The Daisy Bell* quite clearly on her prow.

"The tide," said Farebrother. "She'd have had a job to clear the harbour bar if the water was any lower."

"I didn't think you went out on an ebb-tide," said Ridgeford naively.

"You don't," said Farebrother. "Not without you have a reason." He resumed his fast pace over the shingle, adding, "Unless you're dying, of course."

"Dying?"

"Fishermen always go out with the tide. Didn't you know that? They die at low water . . . ."

The dinghy that had been beached was old, weather-beaten and very waterlogged.

"She's still got her rowlocks with her though," said the lifeboatman professionally. "Funny, that."

"But there's no name on her," noted the policeman with equal but different expertise. "She could have come from anywhere, I suppose?"

"Not anywhere." Farebrother looked the police constable up and down and evidently decided as a result of his appraisal to be helpful. "The tide brings everything down from the north hereabouts."

That hadn't been quite what Ridgeford meant but he did not say so.

"Not up from the south," continued the lifeboatman. "You never find anything that's come up from the south on this shore."

That, thought Ridgeford silently, tied in with a body floating in the estuary of the River Calle.

"Especially with the wind in the west like it's been these past few days," added the other man. "It's a south-east wind that's nobody's friend."

"Yes," said Ridgeford. While Horace Boller almost instinctively knew the state of the tide, so Farebrother would be equally aware of the quarter of the wind. You probably needed to be a farmer to consider the weather as a whole. It was a case of each man to his own trade. Stockbrokers doubtless knew the feel of the market—by the pricking of their thumbs or something—and equally the police . . . Ridgeford wasn't sure what it was that a policeman needed to be constantly aware of . . . There must be something that told a policeman the state of play in the great match "Crime versus Law and Order." The knocking off of helmets, perhaps.

"Against the current that would be, too," continued Farebrother, who was happily unaware of the constable's train of thought.

He made going against the current sound almost as improbable as flying in the face of nature. Had Farebrother been a carpenter, decided Ridgeford to himself, he would have said "against the grain."

Aloud he said to the lifeboatman, "What about this rope at the bow?"

"The painter?" Farebrother looked at the end of the dinghy and the short length of line dangling from it. "She either slipped her mooring or she was untied on purpose."

"Not cut loose or anything like that, then?"

Farebrother shook his head, while Brian Ridgeford limped over to the dinghy. He steadied himself against it as he felt about in his shoe for a stray piece of shingle that had made its way into it.

"Someone'll be along soon looking for it," predicted the lifeboatman, indicating the beached dinghy.

Ridgeford wasn't so sure about that. He found the pebble and removed it.

"With a red face," added Farebrother.

The face that sprang at once to the policeman's mind was white. Dead white was the name that artists' colourmen gave to paint that colour. The owner of that particular face wouldn't be along *Not this tide, nor any tide,* as the poet had it, *For what is sunk will hardly swim, Not with this wind blowing, and this tide.*

"Maybe he will," was all he said to Farebrother though. Ridgeford turned his mind to practicalities, and immediately wished that he had his reference books with him. He wasn't well up in the technicalities of the law yet. Was a dinghy washed up on the foreshore "flotsam" or "jetsam" or the forgotten third of that marine trio "lagan"? More importantly, was it "lost property" or "salvage"?

"Anyways," pronounced Farebrother, resolving that difficulty for him, "we'll keep it here until the owner—whoever he is—turns up. And if he doesn't, you'll let the Receiver of Wrecks and the Department of Trade know, won't you?"

"Of course," said Ridgeford hastily. So the dinghy was none of these things. It was officially a wreck. "I'll get on to him."

"Department of Trade!" Farebrother spat expertly across the shore. "Huh! Trade! I don't suppose anyone there knows the meaning of the word."

"Well . . ." Ridgeford temporised. He was a civil servant himself now and he was beginning to find out that civil servants did know what they were doing.

"And why they couldn't go on calling it the Board of Trade beats me." Farebrother rolled his eyes. "At least everyone knew what you meant then. Department. Huh!"

"They've always got to change things, haven't they?" agreed the young constable briskly. He cast a long glance in the direction of the headland at the south side of the estuary. Some change was for the better. In olden times the good citizens of Marby juxta Mare used to light beacons on this stretch of coast with intent to mislead poor mariners in search of safe landfall. Golden times for the citizens, hard ones for the drowned seafarers. They did say that somewhere out to sea off the headland was the wreck of a merchantman lured to its doom by the ancestors of men like Farebrother . . .

The lifeboatman spat again. "Things should be let alone with, that's what I say. I don't hold with disturbing things that have always been the way they are and I don't mind who knows it."

By the time the constable got back to his home in Edsway his wife was on the look-out for him. He dismounted, undid his bicycle clips and announced portentously, "It's all right, love. It was just an empty boat. Nothing to worry about—it's safely in police hands now."

His helpmeet rather spoilt the effect of this pronouncement by giggling.

"Call police hands safe, do you?" she said saucily. "I don't, Brian Ridgeford."

CHAPTER 7

Gentlemen, I am ordered immediate execution.

"I think it was murder, all right, sir," said Detective Inspector Sloan into the telephone in Dr. Dabbe's office.

"An accident at sea, Sloan," boomed Superintendent Leeyes into his mouthpiece at the police station in Berebury.

Sloan cleared his throat and carried on manfully. "He was killed in a fall from a height first and . . ."

"Washed overboard from an old dinghy," swept on Leeyes.

"And then," continued Sloan with deliberation, "put into the water."

"The dinghy's been found over at Marby juxta Mare," said the superintendent.

"With a copper weight of sorts in his pocket," said Sloan doggedly.

"On the foreshore at Marby," said Leeyes. "Constable Ridgeford has just rung in from Edsway."

There was a flourishing school of thought at the police station which held that the superintendent was deaf. Older hands —more perceptive, perhaps—did not subscribe to this theory. They insisted that the superintendent always heard the things that he wanted to hear all right.

"Why was it murder?" Leeyes asked Sloan suddenly.

"The fall killed him," explained Sloan, "and he certainly wouldn't have got into the water on his own afterwards. Dr. Dabbe's done some X-rays to prove it . . ."

Leeyes grunted. "That's something to be thankful for anyway, Sloan. The last time Dyson and Williams went anywhere near his precious X-ray machine with their cameras I thought we'd never hear the last of it."

Dyson and Williams were the police photographers and there had been a memorable occasion when the pathologist's X-ray equipment had silently ruined all the film in their cameras and about their persons; something they hadn't discovered until after they had shot it . . .

"The fall killed him," repeated Sloan. "I don't know how he fell—I don't know yet who was there when it happened"—his lips tightened as he thought about the young man in the mortuary—"but before I'm done I intend to find out."

"Person or persons unknown," supplied the superintendent, falling back upon an ancient formula. "That'll do for the time being anyway."

"They," continued Sloan with a fine disregard for number and gender, "put his body into the water after that."

"Hrrrrumph."

"Yes, sir," Sloan responded to the sentiment as much as to the sound. "Exactly."

"Don't say it, Sloan."

"No, sir."

"I know the dead can't walk."

"Yes, sir."

"What was that about a copper weight?" The superintendent never forgot anything he wanted to remember either.

"It was a small round lump," said Sloan. "In his pocket."

Leeyes grunted. "Clothes?"

"He didn't have a lot on, sir," replied Sloan. "Shirt and trousers, socks and underclothes . . ."

"Seaboots?" queried Leeyes sharply. "Was he wearing seaboots?"

"No, sir," said Sloan. It had been one of the first things he had looked for. Pincher Martin had had seaboots on. A young Christopher Dennis Sloan had been brought up on the story of Pincher Martin, and when in later life an adult Detective Inspector C. D. Sloan came across a body in the water in the way of business, the poor drowned seaman who had been Pincher Martin came to the front of his mind. Pincher Martin's seaboots hadn't saved him from drowning. "This chap didn't have any seaboots on, sir. Only what I said. Shirt, trousers, socks and underclothes."

"Traceable?" queried Leeyes, who had not been thinking about Pincher Martin.

"Easily," said Sloan.

"Ah!"

"In the first instance, that is," said Sloan.

"Oh?"

"To a well-known store that clothes half the nation."

"But after that?"

"Who's to say?" said Sloan wearily, consciously suppressing an unhappy vision of the routine work it would take to find out.

"Labels not cut out then?" concluded Leeyes briskly.

"Oh, no, sir. We were meant to think that this was a simple case of drowning—if we found the body, that is."

"Oh, we were, were we?" responded Superintendent Leeyes energetically, forgetting for a moment that it had been Dr. Dabbe who had told them it wasn't.

"This dinghy, sir . . ." It was Sloan's turn to do the remembering.

"Old," quoted Leeyes, "but not truly waterlogged. Ridgeford's no seaman but he did notice that much."

"Over at Marby, you said, sir . . ."

"Yes, Sloan." The superintendent's voice faded as he spun round in his swivel chair and consulted the map that hung on the wall. "The tide would have had to take your man round the headland—what's it called?"

"The Cat's Back."

"The Cat's Back and into the estuary of the Calle."

"That," began Sloan carefully, "would mean that he would have had to have been swept out to sea first and then brought in by the tide against the river current."

He heard the swivel chair creak as Leeyes turned back to face the telephone again. "Naturally, Sloan."

"Sir, Dr. Dabbe says that this fellow—whoever he is—hadn't been knocked about by the tide and the river current all that much." Sloan had meant to lead into the point he had to make with the delicacy of a diplomat but in the event he didn't bother. "Not anything like as much as he would have expected."

"But you said he'd been in the water quite a long while," Leeyes pounced.

"Dr. Dabbe said that, sir. Not me," responded Sloan. The superintendent had a tendency which he shared with the ancient Greeks to confuse the messenger with the source of the news. Harbingers had a notoriously bad time with him.

"What you're trying to tell me, Sloan, and I must say you've taken your time about it, is that things aren't quite what they seem."

"That's right, sir."

"There's still this empty dinghy over at Marby," said Superintendent Leeyes down the telephone to the head of his Criminal Investigation Department. "No doubt about that."

"Yes, sir." Sloan got the message. "I'll get over there as soon as I can and have a look at it."

"Doesn't add up, Sloan, does it?"

"No, sir."

"I don't like coincidences," growled Leeyes.

"No, sir," agreed Sloan. No policeman did. Sorting them out from circumstantial evidence in court could get very tricky indeed. Sloan knew—sight unseen—that the superintendent's bushy eyebrows would have come together in a formidable frown as he said that.

"Now what, Sloan?"

"I'm following up the piece of copper, sir, and Dr. Dabbe's lining someone up for me to see, too, who may be able to help with something else . . . a Miss Hilda Collins."

He did not add that that someone was a schoolmistress. Some of Superintendent Leeyes's responses were altogether too predictable.

* * *

Police Constable Brian Ridgeford was addressing himself to a mug of steaming hot tea. One thing Mrs. Ridgeford—good police wife that she was trying too hard to be—had learnt well. That was to put the kettle on the hob and leave it on.

He had dutifully made his report to his Headquarters at Berebury about the beached dinghy and was sitting back considering what to do next. He hadn't forgotten that before he had been diverted over to Marby juxta Mare he had been going to walk up the river bank from Edsway to Collerton, but before that there was his report to be written. One of the tenets at the Police Training School was that—as far as records went—the telephone was no substitute for pen and paper.

"Anything come in while I was out, love?" he asked, conscientiously pulling his report book towards him.

"Hopton's rang," said Mrs. Ridgeford, sitting back and joining him in some tea. She was still at that early stage in their police married life when handing over the message was synonymous with handing over the responsibility. Her sleepless nights would come later.

Brian Ridgeford said, "What's up with Hopton's?" As a rule his wife gave him any messages that had come in almost before he'd got his foot over the threshold, so this one couldn't be too important.

"They want you down there."

Ridgeford frowned. Hopton's was always wanting him down there at the store. Every time a bunch of schoolchildren had been in Mrs. Hopton was convinced that they had stolen things. As far as the weekend sailors and fishermen were concerned—Hopton's prices being distinctly on the high side—all the robbery was on the other side of the counter. And in daylight, too.

"Profits down or something?" he said.

"Boys," said Mrs. Ridgeford succinctly.

So it was to the ship's-chandler by the shore in Edsway that Ridgeford made his way—not too quickly—after he'd had his tea and filled in his report about the dinghy.

Mrs. Hopton was vocal. "There were two of them," she said. "And I had to deal with them myself on account of Hopton being the way he is."

"What did they do?" enquired Ridgeford patiently. Mr.

Hopton spent his life lurking in the little parlour at the back of the shop. He was a little man and his wife was a large woman. No doubt he was the way he was by virtue of being locked in holy wedlock to Mrs. Hopton. It wasn't a fate that he, Brian Ridgeford, would have chosen either.

"Do?" she said, surprised. "They didn't do anything."

"Well, then . . ." Somebody had once tried to explain to his class of new constables the difference between crimes of commission and the sins of omission—the latter mostly, it seemed, to do with their notebooks—but Ridgeford hadn't listened too hard.

"Unless," carried on Mrs. Hopton, "you count trying to make me buy something that wasn't theirs to sell."

"Ah." Ridgeford thought he was beginning to understand. The far end of the ship's-chandler store was devoted to the sale of second-hand equipment.

"At my time of life!" said Mrs. Hopton with every appearance of remorse. "Well, they say there's no fool like an old fool. I should have known better, shouldn't I?"

"Well . . ." temporised the policeman. The theory that all were responsible for their own actions was highly important in law. It was apt to be overlooked in real life.

"Smelt a rat, I should have done, shouldn't I," she sniffed, "as soon as they said where they'd found it."

"But you didn't?" suggested Ridgeford for appearance' sake.

"Not then," said Mrs. Hopton.

"When?" prompted Ridgeford.

"Afterwards," said Mrs. Hopton, challenging him to make something of that. "When they'd gone."

"What made you wonder?"

"When I began to think about it." She shifted her shoulders uneasily. "I wasn't happy."

"About what?"

"Them saying they found it up on the Cat's Back."

"The headland?"

She nodded. "Whoever heard of anyone finding a ship's bell up there?"

"It is a funny place to find anything from a ship," agreed Ridgeford, professionally interested. Common things took place most commonly—he knew that—but it was the uncommon that attracted most police attention. "A bell, did you say?" He imagined that—like policemen's helmets—ships' bells had a symbolic importance all of their own.

"It's a bell all right," said Mrs. Hopton heavily.

Police Constable Ridgeford shifted his gaze in the direction of the jumble of second-hand nautical gear at the end of the store. "Had I better have a look at it, then?"

"Wait a minute," she said. "I've got it safe in the parlour. My husband's keeping an eye on it for me."

Ridgeford was a puzzled man as she turned away.

When she came back it was with a very shabby and encrusted piece of metal and he was more puzzled still.

"It's a bell all right," he agreed after a moment or two, "but you couldn't use it, could you? Not with that crack in its side." There was evidence of some scraping too, from a penknife, he guessed.

"That's what I told the boys," said Mrs. Hopton. "No use to anyone, I said, it being the way it was."

"So," said Ridgeford a trifle impatiently, "what did you want me down here for then?"

"Ships' bells," she said impressively, "have the names of ships on them."

"What about it?"

"They have them cut into the metal so that they last."

"Well?" If Brian Ridgeford was any judge this one had had to last a long time.

"I was curious, you see," she said, looking him straight in the eye. "So I got out a piece of paper and a soft pencil . . ."

"You traced the name," finished the policeman for her.

"Not all of it. Some of it's too far gone."

"You traced some of it," said Ridgeford with heavy patience.

"That's right." Mrs. Hopton was above irony. "I traced some of it and came up with some letters."

"Did you then?" said Ridgeford expressionlessly.

She pulled out a drawer behind the counter. "Do you want to see them?"

Police Constable Brian Ridgeford bent over a piece of grubby paper and read aloud the letters that were discernible. *"E . . . M . . . B . . . A . . . L . . . D. EMBALD?* Is that what it says?"

She gave him a nod of barely suppressed excitement. "I know what the other letters are. Don't you?"

"No," he said. "Tell me."

"C . . . L . . . A . . . R," she said. She was speaking in lowered tones now. "To make *Clarembald."*

"All right then," he conceded. "If you say so—*The Clarembald*. What about it?"

She tossed her head. "I'd forgotten you were new here, Mr. Ridgeford."

"Yes."

"You wouldn't know, I suppose?"

"No."

"Everyone else knows."

"Everyone else knows what?"

She delivered her punch line almost in a whisper. *"The Clarembald* was the name of the ship that went down off Marby all those years ago. Didn't you know that?"

CHAPTER 8

But at present keep your own secret.

Detective Inspector Sloan had not been inside the museum at Calleford since he was a boy.

It was situated inside an old castle that had started life under Edward III as a spanking new bastion against the nearest enemy, degenerated over the years into a prison, and in the twentieth century been revived as a museum. At first Sloan and Crosby followed the way of the ordinary visitor. This led them past glass cases of Romano-British pottery and Jutish finds. They turned left by the vast exhibition of stuffed birds willed by a worthy citizen of bygone days, and kept straight on to the main office through the Darrell Collection of nineteenth-century costume.

There was nothing out of date about the museum's curator.

Mr. Basil Jensen took a quick look at the lump of copper and immediately took over the questioning himself. "Where did you find this?" he demanded excitedly.

"The River Calle."

"The river?" squealed Jensen. "Are you sure?"

"Quite sure," said Sloan. "What is it?"

"A barbary head," said Basil Jensen impatiently. He was a little man who obviously found it hard to keep still. "Where did you say you found it?"

"The river," said Sloan.

"I know that." He danced from one leg to the other. "Whereabouts in the river?"

"Between Edsway and Collerton," said Sloan accurately.

The police usually asked the questions but Sloan was content to let him go on. Sometimes questions were even more revealing than answers. "What's a barbary head?"

"I don't believe it," declared Mr. Jensen with academic ferocity. "Not between Edsway and Collerton."

"No," said Sloan consideringly, "I can see that you might not. What's a barbary head?"

"Now, if you'd said the sea, Inspector . . ."

"Yes?"

"That would have made more sense."

Anything that made sense suited Sloan. Crosby was concentrating more on his surroundings. The museum curator's room was stuffed with improbable objects standing in unlikely juxtaposition. Two vases stood on his desk—one clearly Chinese, one as clearly Indian. Even Sloan's untutored eye could see the difference between them—two whole civilisations summed up in the altered rake of the lip of a vase . . .

"What's a barbary head?" asked Sloan again. Crosby was staring at an oryx whose head—a triumph of the taxidermist's art—was at eye level on the wall. The oryx stared unblinkingly back at him.

"A single head of barbary copper," said Basil Jensen authoritatively, "moulded into a circular shape." He blinked. "Any the wiser?"

"No," said Sloan truthfully.

"An ingot, then."

"Ah."

"It was the way they used to transport copper in the old days."

"I see."

Mr. Jensen pointed to the copper object. "You'd get tons and tons of it like this. A man could move it with a shovel, you see. Easier than shifting great lumps that needed two men to lift them."

"What sort of old days?" asked Sloan cautiously.

"Let's not beat about the bush," said Mr. Jensen.

Sloan was all in favour of that.

"Mid-eighteenth century," said the museum curator impressively.

"Make a note of that, Crosby," said Sloan.

"Mid-eighteenth century," repeated Mr. Jensen.

"That would be about 1750, wouldn't it, sir?" said Sloan. "Give or take a year or two."

"Or five," said Mr. Jensen obscurely. He tapped the barbary head. "And at a guess . . ."

"Yes?"

"This has been in the water since then." He thrust his chin forward. "If you don't believe me, Inspector, take it to Greenwich. They'll know there." He suddenly looked immensely cunning. "There's something else they'll be able to tell you, too."

"What's that, sir?"

"Whether it's been in salt water or fresh all these years."

Sloan said, "I think I may know the answer to that, sir."

The museum curator nodded and pointed to the piece of copper. "And I think, Inspector, that I know the answer to this."

"You do, sir?"

"Someone's found *The Clarembald.*" He spoke almost conversationally now. "She was an East Indiaman, you know . . ."

Across the years Sloan caught the sudden whiff of blackboard chalk at the back of his nostrils and he was once again in the classroom of a long-ago schoolmaster. The man—a rather precise, dry man—had been trying to convey to a class of boys that strange admixture of trade, empire-building and corruption that had made the East India Company what it was. He'd been a "chalk and talk" schoolmaster but one rainy afternoon he'd made John Company and the investigation of Robert Clive and the impeachment of Warren Hastings all come alive to his class.

"Someone's found her," said Jensen.

They'd been all ears, those boys, especially when the teacher had come to that macabre incident in British history that everybody knows. It was strange, thought Sloan, that out of a crowded historical past "when all else be forgot" everyone always remembered the Black Hole of Calcutta.

"We knew it would happen one day," said the museum curator. "In fact," he admitted, "we'd heard a rumour. Nothing you could put your finger on, you know . . ."

"Ah."

"And people have been in making enquiries," said Jensen.

Sloan leaned forward. "You wouldn't happen to know which people, sir, would you?"

"They don't leave their names," said Jensen drily. "And we get a lot of casual enquirers, you know."

"Short, dark and young?" said Sloan.

Jensen shook his head. "Tallish, brown hair and not as young as all that."

"This ship," said Sloan. "You know all about it then?"

"Bless you, Inspector, yes." Jensen started to pace up and down. "It's perfectly well documented. And it's all here in the museum for anyone to look up. She was lured to her doom by wreckers in the winter of 1755 . . ."

"The evil that men do lives after them," murmured Sloan profoundly.

Jensen's response was immediate. "Yes, indeed, Inspector. We see a lot of that in the museum world."

Sloan hadn't thought of that.

Jensen waved a hand. "I daresay that I can tell you what *The Clarembald* was carrying too . . ."

Quinquireme of Nineveh from distant Ophir . . .

"We have a copy of the ship's manifest here," said Jensen, jerking to a standstill. "I daresay the East India Office will have something about it too." He pointed to the barbary head and went on enthusiastically, "And if she wasn't carrying a load of copper ingots I'll eat my hat. Mind you, Inspector, that won't have been all her cargo by a long chalk. She'll have had a great many other good things on board."

Sloan motioned to Crosby to take a note.

"A great many other things," said the museum curator, "that certain people would like to have today."

"Gold?" suggested Sloan simply.

Topazes and cinnamon, and gold moidores, it had been in the poem.

Mr. Jensen gave a quick frown. "Gold, certainly. Don't forget it was used as currency then. But it won't be so much the gold as the guns that they'll be going for today."

"Guns?" said Sloan. "Guns before gold?" He was faintly disappointed. Pieces of eight had a swashbuckling ring to them.

"They're easier to find underwater," said Jensen. "And if I remember rightly she had a pair of Demi-Culverin on board and some twelve pounders."

Sloan was struck by a different thought. "Armed merchantmen were nothing new, then?"

"If you worked in a museum, Inspector, you'd realise that there is nothing new under the sun."

"Quite so," said Sloan.

Mr. Jensen came back very quickly to the matter in hand. "There are treasure-seekers, Inspector, who would blow her out of the water for her guns and not care that they were destroying priceless marine archeology. Do you realise that everything that comes out of an underwater find should be kept underwater?"

"She doesn't," observed Sloan moderately, "appear to have been blown out of the water yet."

"Matter of time," said Jensen, resuming his restless pacing. "Only a matter of time. Depends entirely on who knows she's been found and how quickly they act."

"I can see that, sir." There were villains everywhere. You learned that early in the police force. "There must be something that can be done about stopping her being damaged."

"Done? Oh, yes," said Jensen. "For those in peril in the sea, Inspector, we can get a Department of Trade protection order making it an offence to interfere with the wreck or carry out unlicenced diving or salvage." He turned on his heel suddenly and faced Sloan. "But we'd need to know where she was. How did you say you'd come by this barbary head?"

"I didn't," said Sloan quietly, "and I'm not going to."

* * *

Elizabeth Busby felt strangely relaxed and comforted after her cry at the graveside. She was sure that her aunt would have understood her need to leave the house and seek out a quiet spot in the out of doors. Celia Mundill would have understood the tears too—there was a marvellous release to be had in tears. And Collerton graveyard was certainly quiet enough—it was a fine and private place for tears, in fact.

True, Horace Boller from Edsway had rowed past on his way upstream but he hadn't disturbed her thoughts at all. Perhaps this was because those thoughts were still too inchoate and unformed to admit intrusion from an outside source. Perhaps it was only because—more mundanely—she hadn't liked to lift a tear-stained face for it to be seen by the man who had been going by.

She felt much better in the open air; she was sure about that. Collerton House had begun to oppress her since Celia Mundill had died—it wasn't the same without her warm presence, ill as she had been. It wasn't the same either—subconsciously she stiffened her shoulders—since Peter Hinton had so precipitately taken his departure. There was no use baulking at the fact—no matter how hard she tried to think of other things, in the end her thoughts always came back to Peter Hinton.

She had felt at the time and she still felt now that a note left on the table in the hall was no way for a real man to break with his affianced. If he had felt the way he said he did, then the very least he could have done was to have told her so—face to face. A note left behind on the hall table beside the signet ring she had given him was the coward's way.

For the thousandth time she took the folded paper which Peter Hinton had written out of her pocket and—for the thousandth time—considered it. Its message was loud and clear. It could scarcely have been shorter or balder either.

It's no go. Forgive me. P.

There was not a word of explanation as to why a man who had quite unequivocally declared that he wanted to marry her should suddenly leave a note like that. Time and time again she had turned it over to see if there had been more—anything—written on the back but there wasn't.

There still wasn't.

She had resolved not to keep on and on reading the note—and forgotten how many times she had made the resolution. She'd broken it every day. She didn't know why she needed to look at it anyway. It wasn't as if she didn't know what it said. Sadly she folded it up again and put it away.

She sat back on her heels then, more at peace with herself than she'd been all day. There was something very peaceful about the churchyard—you could begin to see what it was about a churchyard that had moved Thomas Gray to write his elegy and why her aunt hadn't wanted to be cremated. There was something very soothing, too, about the sound of the water lapping away at the edge of the churchyard grass. Gray hadn't had that at—where was it? Stoke Poges.

Elizabeth reached over and picked out the flowers that she had brought with her on her last visit. They were fading now. That gave her something to do with her hands and that was soothing too. As she carefully started to arrange the roses in the vase she began to understand why it was that her aunt's husband had been so insistent about his wife's grave being within the sound of the water.

"She'd spent all her life by the river," he'd said, immediately selecting the plot that was closest to the river's edge.

The sexton had murmured something about flooding.

"But she loved the sound of the river," Frank Mundill had insisted.

The sexton had hitched his shoulder. "You won't like it in winter, Mr. Mundill."

Architects spend at least half their working lives persuading recalcitrant builders to do what architect and client want and Frank Mundill had had to prove his skill in this field in the five minutes that followed.

"It couldn't be too near the river for her," he had said.

"The first time the Calle comes up," sniffed the sexton obstinately, "you'll be on to me. You see."

"I won't," undertook Frank Mundill.

"And there won't be anything I can do then," said the man as if he hadn't spoken.

"I shan't want you to do anything."

"It'll be too late then," said the man obdurately. "Mark my words."

"My wife was born over there, remember." Frank Mundill had waved a hand in the direction of Collerton House. He introduced a firmer tone into his voice. "She loved this river."

His gesture had reminded Elizabeth Busby of something and she had taken herself off at that point to have a look at her grandparents' grave. That was over by the church—not far from the west door. And next to it was the polished marble monument to her great grandparents. Gordon Camming—he who had invented the Camming valve—had made it clear that he intended to found a dynasty too. He'd bought half a dozen plots around his own tomb; the sexton hadn't hesitated to remind Frank Mundill of this.

The word "dynasty" had started up another unhappy train of thought in her mind at the time, not unconnected with Peter Hinton, and she had drifted back to the river's edge where the exchange between Frank Mundill and the sexton was drawing to a close. By the time she had reached the two men, the site of the plot for the grave of her aunt had been agreed upon and the sexton, if still not happy about it, at least mollified.

"She'll be content here," she heard Celia Mundill's widower insisting as she drew closer.

Elizabeth hoped then and hoped now as she tended the flowers on the grave that this was true. It was still summertime, of course, and flooding was a long way from her mind as she took away the last of the dead flowers from her previous visit. She sat back on her heels while she carefully picked out the best rose for the centre position. Her aunt had known she would never see this year's Fantin-Latour roses on the bush—she'd told Elizabeth so in spite of all Dr. Tebot had said—but there was no reason, she told herself fiercely, why she shouldn't have them on her grave.

As she placed each succeeding stem of the double blush-pink clusters of flowers in the grave's special frost-proof vase she began to see why it was that this particular rose had been such a favourite—and not only of Celia Mundill but of Henri Fantin-Latour and the old Dutch flower painters—of real artists, in fact.

Involuntarily her lips tightened into a smile.

There was a family joke about the word "artist." Grandfather Camming had called himself an artist and filled canvas upon canvas to prove it. The family had tacitly agreed therefore that he must be known as an artist. Other artists—those who did improve as time went by, those whose pictures were fought over by art galleries—even those whose paintings were bought with an eye to the future—deserved to be distinguished from Richard Camming and his amateur efforts. They had been known—in the family and out of earshot of Richard Camming—as real artists.

"Poor Grandfather!" she thought. Time and money weren't what made a painter. "Nor," she added fairly in her mind, "was application." Grandfather Camming had certainly applied himself. She gave a little, silent giggle to herself. Richard Camming had cheerfully applied paint to every canvas in sight.

As Elizabeth placed the roses in the vase she was conscious of how the lively shell-pink of the centre of the flower made a fine splash of colour against the newly turned earth. She would have liked to have had that bare earth covered in stone or even grass but the sexton said it had to stay the way it was until it had settled. Frank Mundill didn't seem worried about the bare earth either. When she had mentioned it to him later he had said he was still thinking about the right monumental design and so she had left the subject well alone.

She sat back on her heels for a moment to consider her handiwork in flower arrangement. She hoped it wouldn't flood in this corner of the churchyard but you never could tell with the River Calle. The river seemed to have a will of its own. Way, way inland—above Calleford, and almost as far inland as the town of Luston—it was a docile stream, little more than a rivulet, in fact. By the time it got to Calleford itself it was bigger, of course, but it was tamed there by city streets and bridges, to say nothing of the odd sluice gate.

Once west of the county town, though, and out onto the flat land in the middle of the county—those very same low-lying fields in which Grandfather Camming had painted during his Constable period—the River Calle broadened and steadily grew into a force of water to be reckoned with. The bends in its course through Collerton towards Edsway and the sea it seemed to regard as a challenge to its strength. In spring and autumn, that is.

Her flowers arranged and her tears dried and forgotten for the time being, Elizabeth Busby rose to her feet and dusted off her knees. She decided that she would walk back to the house along the river bank. It was a slightly longer way back to Collerton House than by the paved road but what was time to her now?

She slipped out of the little kissing gate that led from the churchyard onto the river walk feeling rather as if she had stepped out of a William Morris painting—or was it another of the Pre-Raphaelites who had been so fond of having girls stationed prettily beside a river as they put brush to canvas? Perhaps it was Millais? Not Baron Leighton, surely? She always felt a little self-conscious when she was walking along the river bank with a wooden gardening trug over one arm. At least she didn't have a Victorian parasol in the other.

It was while she was walking back along the path on the river bank and rounding the bend that matched the curve of the river that the boathouse at the bottom of the garden of Collerton House came into view.

Someone, she noticed in a detached way, had left the doors of the boathouse open.

CHAPTER 9

See my courage is out.

Detective Inspector Sloan and Detective Constable Crosby made their way back to the pathologist's mortuary. They found the pathologist in his secretary's room, there talking to a squarish woman with shaggy eyebrows and cropped hair. Rita, the pathologist's secretary, was there too. She was a slim girl whose eyebrows showed every sign of having had a lot of loving care and attention lavished upon them. Dr. Dabbe introduced the older woman to the policemen as Miss Hilda Collins.

"We've met before," she announced, acknowledging them with a quick jerk of her head.

Sloan bowed slightly.

"I never forget a face," declared Miss Collins.

"It's a gift," said Sloan, and he meant it. For his part Sloan remembered her too. Miss Collins was the biology mistress at the Berebury High School for Girls. "I wish we had more policemen who didn't forget faces," he said—and he meant that too. What with Identikits, memory banks and computer-assisted this and that, the man on the beat didn't really have to remember any more what villains looked like. It was a pity.

At the other side of the room Constable Crosby was exhibiting every sign of trying to commit Rita's face to memory. Sloan averted his eyes.

"Miss Collins," said the pathologist easily, "is an expert."

"I see." Sloan remained cautious. If his years in the Force had taught him anything, it was that experts were a breed on their own. Put them in the witness box and you never knew what they were going to say next. They could make or mar a case, too. Irretrievably. There was only one thing worse than one expert and that was two. Then they usually differed. "May I ask on what?" he said politely.

"Good question," said Dr. Dabbe. "I must say I'd rather like to know myself. It's in the lab . . . this way." He led them through from his secretary's room into the small laboratory that Sloan knew existed alongside the post-mortem room. "I called him Charley because he travelled," said the pathologist obscurely.

"With the body, I think you said," murmured Miss Collins gruffly.

"It was my man Burns who said that," said Dr. Dabbe. "He found it wriggling inside the man's shirt. That was still very wet."

"He found what . . ." began Sloan peremptorily, and then stopped.

The pathologist was pointing to a wide-necked retort that was almost full of water. Swimming happily about in it was a small creature. "Burns said they call it a 'screw' in Scotland," he said.

As if to prove the point the creature wriggled suddenly sideways. It was a dull greenish-yellow colour and quite small.

"It's still alive," said Detective Constable Crosby unnecessarily.

"That proves something," said Miss Collins immediately. "What's it in?"

"Aqua destillata," said the pathologist who belonged to the old school which felt that the Latin language and the profession of medicine should always go together.

Sloan made a mental note that sturdily included the words "distilled water." Latin used where English would do always made him think of Merlin and spells.

Miss Collins advanced on the specimen in the glass. "It's one of the Crustacea," she said.

"That's what I thought," said Dr. Dabbe.

"Amphipod, of course," announced Miss Collins. "The

order is known as 'Sand-hoppers' although few live in the sand and even fewer still hop."

There were inconsistencies in law, too. Sloan had stopped worrying about them now but when he had been a younger man they'd sometimes come between him and a good night's sleep.

"You'll find it demonstrates negative heliotropism very nicely," Miss Collins said.

If she had been speaking in a foreign tongue, Detective Inspector Sloan would have been allowed to bring in an interpreter at public expense. And as far as Sloan was concerned she might as well have been.

The pathologist must have understood her, though, because he pushed the jar half into and half out of the rays of sunlight falling on the laboratory bench. Whatever it was in the water—fish or insect—jerked quickly away from that part of the jar and scuttled off into such dimmer light as it could find.

"We do that with the third form," said Miss Collins in a kindly way, "to teach them phototropism."

Dr. Dabbe was unabashed while Miss Collins bent down for an even closer look. "The family Gammaridae," she pronounced.

Detective Constable Crosby abandoned any attempt to record this. He too bent down and looked at the creature. "Doesn't it look big through the glass?" he said.

"You get illusory magnification from curved glass with water in it," the pathologist informed him absently.

Both Miss Collins and Crosby were still peering, fascinated, at the glass retort and its contents. Some dentists, Sloan was reminded, had tanks with goldfish swimming in them in their waiting rooms. The theory was that patients were soothed by watching fish move about. *In a cool curving world he lies* . . . no, that was the river in Rupert Brooke's *Fish* but no doubt the principle was the same. There were insomniacs, too, who had them by their beds. The considering of fish swimming was said to lower tension all round.

He looked across at Detective Constable Crosby. He didn't want his assistant's tension lowered any more.

"Have you got a note of that, Crosby?" he barked unfairly.

Miss Collins said, "It can't osmoregulate, you know, Inspector."

Sloan didn't know and said so.

"True estuarine species can," declared Miss Collins.

Sloan did not enjoy being blinded with Science.

"Gammarus pulex, Inspector, is a good example of a biological indicator."

Sloan said he was very glad to hear it.

The pathologist leaned forward eagerly and said, "So Charley here . . ."

"I'm not at all sure that I can tell you its sex," said Miss Collins meticulously. She raised her head from considering the water creature and asked clearly, "Is sex important?"

Sloan stiffened. If Crosby said that sex was always important then he, Detective Inspector Sloan, his superior officer, would put him on report there and then . . . murder case or not. Detective Constable Crosby, however, continued to be absorbed by half an inch of wriggling crustacean and it was Sloan who found himself answering her.

"No," he said into the silence.

He felt that sounded prim and expanded on it.

"Not as far as I know," he added.

That sounded worse.

He lost his nerve altogether and launched into further speech.

"In this particular case," he added lamely.

Miss Collins looked extremely scientific. *"Gammarus pulex* enjoys a curious sort of married life."

As a quondam bobby on the beat Sloan could have told her that that went for quite a slice of the human population too.

"But," she carried on, "you don't get the really intricate sex reversal as in—say—the Epicarids."

Sloan was glad to hear it. If there was one thing that the law had not really been able to bend its mind round yet, it was sex reversal.

"Can you eat it?" asked Detective Constable Crosby.

Miss Collins gave a hortatory cough while Sloan had to agree to himself that food did come a close second to sex most of the time. She shook her head and said, "Its common name of freshwater shrimp is a complete misnomer."

In the end it was Sloan who cut the cackle and got down to the horses. "What you're trying to tell us, miss, is that this . . . this . . . whatever it is . . . is a freshwater species, not a sea one."

"That's what I said, Inspector," she agreed patiently. "*Gammarus pulex* can't live in sea water and that's what makes it a good biological indicator."

"So," said Sloan slowly and carefully, "the body didn't come in from the sea."

"I don't know about the body," said the biologist with precision, "but I can assure you that *Gammarus pulex* didn't."

"Are you telling me," asked Sloan, anxious to have at least one thing clear in his mind, "that it—this thing here—would have died in sea water then?"

"I am," she said with all the lack of equivocation of the true scientist on sound territory covered by natural laws.

A little hush fell in the laboratory.

Then Sloan said heavily, "We'd better get our best feet forward then, hadn't we?"

Perhaps in their own way policemen were amphipods too.

Or amphiplods.

Gammarus pulex scuttled sideways across the bottom of the glass vessel as he spoke.

He'd have to prise Crosby away from that jar if he watched it much longer. He was practically mesmerized by it as it was.

"We'll have to go up river," Sloan announced to nobody in particular. He turned. "Come along, Crosby."

Detective Constable Crosby straightened up at last. "We might find some Dead Man's Fingers, too, sir, mightn't we?"

"*Alcyonium digitatum*," said Dr. Dabbe.

"Not in fresh water," said Miss Collins promptly. "Dead Man's Fingers are animals colonial that like the sea-shore."

Sloan didn't say anything at all.

* * *

Police Constable Brian Ridgeford was confused. He had duly reported the finding of the ship's bell to Berebury Police

Station and had in fact brought it back to his home with him. Home in the case of a country constable was synonymous with place of work. His wife was less than enchanted when he set the bell down on the kitchen table.

"Take that out to the shed," commanded Mrs. Ridgeford immediately.

Ridgeford picked it up again.

"What is it anyway?" she asked. "It looks like a bell to me."

"It is a bell," he said. That sounded like one of those childhood conundrums that came in Christmas crackers.

Question: When is a door not a door?

Answer: When it's ajar.

When was a bell not a bell?

When it was treasure trove. Or was it only that when it—whatever it was—had been hidden by the original owner with the intention of coming back for it? Not lost at sea. He would have to look that up. He felt a little self-conscious anyway about using the words "treasure trove" to his wife.

"It's a ship's bell," he said lamely.

"I can see that."

"It's stolen property, too, I think." He cleared his throat and added conscientiously, "Although I don't rightly know about that for sure." Unfortunately when he'd telephoned the police station he'd been put through to Superintendent Leeyes. This had compounded his confusion.

"Dirty old thing," she said, giving it a closer look.

"I think it could be lagan as well."

"I don't care what it is, I'm not having anything like that in my clean kitchen." She looked up suspiciously. "What's lagan anyway?"

"Goods or wreckage lying on the bed of the sea."

She sniffed. "I'm still not having it in here."

"Mind you," he said carefully, "in law things aren't always what they seem." Being in the police force gave a man a different view of the legal system. "In law an oyster is a wild animal."

"Get away with you, Brian Ridgeford."

"It's true. A judge said so."

"Oh, a judge." Brenda Ridgeford hadn't been a policeman's wife for very long, but long enough to be critical of judges and their judgements.

"Sat for a day in court they did to decide."

"The law's an ass, then," she giggled.

"An ass is a domestic animal," said her husband promptly.

She gave him a very sly look indeed. "So's a wife or have you forgotten?"

In the nature of things it was a little while before the ship's bell was moved out to the shed and Brian Ridgeford was able to concentrate on his duties again. These centred on finding the two boys who had taken the bell into the ship's-chandler in Edsway.

To Mrs. Hopton, "boy" was a species not an individual.

Of their age she had been uncertain.

Of their appearance she could tell him nothing beyond that they had been scruffy—but then these days all boys were scruffy, weren't they?

But she was convinced and Hopton—even with him being the way he was—agreed with her here—that they had been up to no good.

On being pressed to describe them she had advanced the view that one had been taller than the other.

Brian Ridgeford had received this gem of observation in silence.

Mrs. Hopton had cogitated still further and eventually disgorged the fact that one of them had called the other "Terry."

As he picked up his helmet and made for the door, Constable Ridgeford reflected that it wasn't a lot to go on. On the other hand with Jack the Ripper they hadn't even had a name.

* * *

"The boathouse?" said Frank Mundill when Elizabeth Busby met him in the hall.

"You'd better go down and have a look," she said, putting her flower trug down on the settle.

"What about the boat? Has that gone?"

"I didn't look inside . . ." Her hands fell helplessly to her sides. "I'm sorry, Frank. I should have done, shouldn't I? The trouble is that I'm still not thinking straight."

"Don't worry." He gave a jerky nod. "I'll go down there now and see what's happened."

"Anyway," recollected Elizabeth, pulling herself together with an effort, "I didn't have a key to the little door on the garden side."

He turned to the drawer in the hall table over which hung Richard Camming's venture into the style of David Allan, the Scottish Hogarth. "That should be here somewhere." He rummaged about until he found it. "Here we are."

"I couldn't see if there was a lot of damage," said Elizabeth.

He essayed a small smile. "Let's hope the boat's all right, anyway. Your father likes his fishing, doesn't he?"

"He'll be looking forward to it," she said. That was quite true. Her father would go straight down to the river with rod and line as soon as he arrived.

In the end Elizabeth walked down through the grounds of Collerton House to the river's edge with him.

"Vandals," Frank Mundill said bitterly, regarding the damaged doors from the river bank. "They must have taken a bar to the lock."

Elizabeth nodded.

"Someone had a go at it last year, too, when we were at my sister's," he said. "I've already had it repaired once."

"I remember," she said, although what she chiefly remembered about the visits of Frank and Celia Mundill to Calleford had been that this year's one had marked the beginning of her aunt's last illness. Frank Mundill's sister was married to a doctor in single-handed general practice there. The architect and his wife Celia had made a habit over the years at each Easter of looking after a locum tenens for the Calleford couple while the doctor and his wife had a well-earned holiday. Celia Mundill hadn't been well then—that was when she had had a really bad attack of stomach pain and vomiting, though it hadn't been her first. Then she'd had an X-ray at Calleford Hospital. She'd gone steadily downhill after that . . .

"Let's go inside," said Mundill.

He unlocked the landward doors of the boathouse and led the way in. His footsteps echoed eerily on the hardstanding inside while the water lapped at its edge. The only light came from a small fan light and the open doors. There was quite enough light though in which to see that the boat was gone.

"Thieves as well as vandals," said Mundill, regarding the empty water.

"Nothing's safe these days, is it?" commented Elizabeth Busby, conscious even as she said it that the remark was both trite and beyond her years. She must be careful. At this rate she'd be old before her time.

"And where do you suppose the fishing boat's got to?" asked Mundill.

"Edsway?" she suggested.

"More likely the open sea," he said gloomily.

"Unless it's fetched up on Billy's Finger."

"We'd have heard," he said.

"So we would."

"No," he said, shaking his head, "we shan't see that boat again."

"Pity."

"Yes," he said, "your father won't be pleased." He sighed. "And neither will the insurance company."

Her eyes turned automatically to the walls of the boathouse. Along them rested the family's collection of fishing rods. "Is there anything gone from there too?"

He looked up and then shook his head. "Doesn't look like it, does it? No, I daresay the boat went for a joy ride."

"When?" She very nearly added "before or after," but she stopped herself in time. In her mind she was still dating everything that happened as before or after that dreadful week of the death of her aunt and the departure of Peter Hinton.

Frank Mundill shook his head yet again. "I don't know when. I don't use the river path all that often. I usually go the other way."

"So do I."

He gave the boathouse a last look round. "There's not a lot that we can do about it now anyway. Come along back to the house and I'll ring the constable at Edsway. Not that that'll do a lot of good. Can't see the police being interested, can you?"

CHAPTER 10

To be hang'd with you.

What at this moment was interesting the police—the police as personified by Superintendent Leeyes, that is—was something quite different.

"Ridgeford rang in," said Leeyes to Detective Inspector Sloan across his office desk, "excited as a schoolgirl."

"What about?" It wouldn't do, of course. Sloan was agreed about that. Being as excited as anybody wouldn't do at all if Ridgeford was going to make a good policeman. Sometimes the very calm of the police officer was the only thing going for him in a really tight situation.

"The wreck off Marby," said Leeyes.

Sloan's head came up with a jerk. If a certain copper ingot had come from there too, then Sloan was prepared to be interested in it as well.

"The Clarembald," said Leeyes, "wrecked by the people of Marby in olden times."

"At least," said Sloan, "that's one crime we don't have to worry about now." Idly he wondered what the exact wording of the charge against the wrecker would have been. There hadn't been a lot of call for it down at the station since sail went out and steam came in. Perhaps it wasn't even in the book any more. "Lighting beacons with intent to deceive" didn't quite seem to fit the gravity of the crime.

"The ship's bell has come ashore," Leeyes told him.

"Has it indeed?" said Sloan. "Well, well."

"As well as that brass weight you said was on the dead body . . ."

"Copper ingot," murmured Sloan, his mind on other things. "How long ago do you suppose *The Clarembald* was found?"

"I wouldn't know about that," responded Leeyes irritably. "All I can tell you is that Ridgeford's only just come across the bell."

"I should have thought," said Sloan slowly, "that we should have heard, sir, if it wasn't very lately."

Leeyes grunted. "Good news gets about."

"We mostly do hear," said Sloan. It was true. The police usually heard about good fortune as well as bad. For one thing good fortune could be as dangerous to the recipient as the reverse . . . Sloan pulled himself up with a jerk. He was beginning to think like a latter-day Samuel Smiles now.

Leeyes grunted again.

"Besides, sir, presumably the coroner would have had to know if anything had been found, wouldn't he?"

"Coroners," pronounced Leeyes obscurely, "only know what they're told."

"Yes, sir."

"And all I know," said Leeyes flatly, "is what my officers choose to tell me."

"Quite so, sir."

"And that's not a lot, Sloan, is it?"

"The young man's body was put into the river where the water is fresh," responded Sloan absently, answering the implication rather than the question.

"And if that's not enough," continued Leeyes, aggrieved, "we've got Ridgeford playing pirates."

"He's having quite a day for a beginner, isn't he?" said Sloan. "A body and buried treasure."

"Hrrrrumph," said Leeyes.

"He'll have to remember today, won't he," said Sloan, "when the routine begins to bite."

Leeyes sniffed. "He'd have me out there, Sloan, if he could . . ."

Sloan didn't say anything at all to that.

"Mind you, Sloan, with my background I've always been interested in the sea."

Sloan could see where this was leading.

"Did I," said Leeyes, "ever tell you how we got ashore at Walcheren?"

"Yes," said Sloan with perfect truth. Nobody had been spared that story. Recitals of the superintendent's wartime experiences were well known and were to be avoided at all costs. He didn't even "stoppeth one in three." Every officer on station got them.

"Bit of a splash," said Leeyes with the celebrated British understatement favoured by men of action in a tight corner.

Detective Inspector Sloan could see where this was leading, too. In another two minutes Superintendent Leeyes would have constituted himself Berebury's currently ranking expert on underwater archeology. And then where would they be?

"I'll see Ridgeford presently, sir," Sloan said firmly, "and find out about the ship's bell too."

"And this dinghy that he keeps on about over at Marby," said Leeyes. "You won't forget that, will you, Sloan?"

"No, sir, I'll see about that as soon as I can . . ." But before that, come wind, come weather, he had every intention of going up the River Calle.

* * *

A little later a police car with Detective Constable Crosby at the wheel and Detective Inspector Sloan in the front passenger seat swept out of the police station at Berebury for the second time that afternoon. The driver negotiated the traffic islands with impatience and then steered past the town's multi-storey car park. Eventually he swung the car onto the open road and out into the Calleshire countryside. In a wallet on the back seat of the police car was a hastily drawn-up list of everyone who lived beside the River Calle on both sides of the river east of Billing Bridge.

"There's a note of the riparian owners, too, sir," said Detective Constable Crosby, "whoever they are when they're at home."

"The fishing rights belong to them," said Sloan.

"Oh, the fishing . . ." said Crosby, putting his foot down.

"There's no hurry," said Sloan as the car picked up speed.

"Got a catch a murderer," said Crosby, "haven't we?"

That, at least, decided Sloan to himself, had the merit of reducing the case to its simplest. And he had to admit that that was not unwelcome after a session with Superintendent Leeyes . . .

"Chance would be a fine thing," he said aloud.

"Someone did for him," said the constable. "He didn't get the way he was and where he was on his own."

"True." As inductive logic went it wasn't a very grand conclusion but it would do. "Can you go any further?"

"We've got to get back to the water," said Crosby, crouching forward at the wheel like Toad of Toad Hall.

Sloan nodded. In all fairness he had to admit that what Crosby had said was true. All the action so far had been in water . . . He said, "What do we know so far?"

"Very little, sir."

It was not the right answer from pupil to mentor.

In the Army mounting a campaign was based on the useful trio of "information, intention, method." He wasn't going to get very far discussing these with Crosby if the detective constable baulked at "information."

"Could you," said Sloan with a hortatory cough, "try to think of why a body killed in a fall should be found in water?"

"Because it couldn't be left where it fell," responded Crosby promptly.

"Good. Go on."

"I don't know why it couldn't be left where it fell, sir," said the constable. "But if it could have been left, then it would have been, wouldn't it?"

"True."

"Heavy things, bodies . . ."

Sloan nodded. What Crosby had just said was simple and irrefutable but it wasn't enough. "Keep going," he said.

Crosby's eyebrows came together in a formidable frown. "Where it fell could have been too public," he said.

"That's a point," said Sloan.

"And it might have been found too soon," suggested Crosby after further thought.

"Very true," said Sloan. "Anything else?"

"Where it was found might give us a lead on who killed him."

"Good, good," said Sloan encouragingly. "Now, why put the body in the water?"

But Crosby's fickle interest had evaporated.

"Why," repeated Sloan peremptorily, "put the body in the water?"

Crosby took a hand off the steering wheel and waved it. "Saves digging a hole," he said simply.

"Anything else?" said Sloan.

Crosby thought in silence.

"Are there," said Sloan tenaciously, "any other good reasons why a body should be put in the water?" It looked as if they were going to have to make bricks without straw in this case anyway . . .

Crosby continued to frown prodigiously but to no effect.

"It is virtually impossible to hide a grave," pronounced Detective Inspector Sloan academically.

"Yes, sir."

"And," continued Sloan, "the disposal of a murdered body therefore presents a great problem to the murderer."

"Yes, sir."

"It often," declared Sloan in a textbook manner, "presents a greater problem than committing the actual murder."

"Murder's easy," said Crosby largely.

"Not of an able-bodied young man," Sloan reminded him. "Of women and children and the old, perhaps." He considered the tempting vista opened up by this thought—but unless you were psychotic you murdered for a reason, and reason and easy victim did not always go hand in hand.

The constable changed gear while Sloan considered the various ways in which someone could be persuaded into falling from a height. "He must have been taken by surprise on the edge of somewhere," he said aloud.

"Pushed, anyway," said Crosby.

"Yes," agreed Sloan. "If he'd fallen accidentally, he could have been left where he fell."

"Shoved when he wasn't looking, then," concluded Crosby.

"We have to look for a height with a concealed bottom . . ."

"Pussy's down the well," chanted Crosby.

"And not too conspicuous a top," said Sloan.

"Somewhere where the victim would have a reason for going with the murderer," suggested Crosby.

"He'd have had to have been pretty near the brink of somewhere even then," said Sloan. "That's what parapets are for."

"With someone he trusted then," said Crosby.

"With someone he didn't think there was any need to be afraid of," said Sloan with greater precision. He reached over to the back seat for the list of riparian owners. He wasn't expecting any trouble from them. Fishing in muddy waters was a police prerogative and he didn't care who knew it.

* * *

Horace Boller was as near to being contented with his day as he ever allowed himself to be. As he pushed his rowing boat off from the shore at Edsway—Horace had never paid a mooring fee in his life—he reflected on how an ill wind always blew somebody good.

He would have known that his two passengers were policemen even if the older one hadn't said so straightaway. There was a certain crispness about him that augured the backing of an institution. Horace Boller was an old hand at discerning those whose brief authority was bolstered by the hidden reserves of an organisation like the police force and the Army—the vicar came in a class of his own—and those who threw their weight about because they were merely rich.

Horace had quite a lot to do with the merely rich on Saturdays and Sundays. The rich who liked sailing were very important in the economy of Edsway. From Monday to Friday they disappeared from Horace's ken—presumably to get richer still in a mysterious place known simply as the city. Horace himself had never been there and when someone had once equated the city with London—which he had been to—Horace's mind failed to make the connection.

Nevertheless Sunday evenings always saw a great exodus of weekenders, albeit tired and happy and sometimes quite weather-beaten, from Edsway back to the city. The following Friday evening—in summertime anyway—saw them return, pale and exhausted, from their labours in the town and raring for a weekend's pleasure—and sunburn in the country. Horace, whose own skin bore a close resemblance to old and rather dirty creased leather, could never decide whether sunburn was a pleasure or a pain for the weekenders.

As a rule therefore Horace Boller only had Saturdays and Sundays in which to pursue the important business of getting rich himself. This accounted for his contentment this day which was neither a Saturday nor a Sunday. Extra money for one trip on a weekday and at the expense of Her Majesty's Government to boot was a good thing; extra money twice was a cause for rejoicing. Not that anyone would have guessed this from Horace Boller's facial expression. His countenance bore its usual surly look and his mind was totally bent on the business of deriving as much financial benefit as he could from this particular expedition—as it was on every other excursion which he undertook.

He gave his starboard oar an expert twist to get the boat properly out into the water and then set about the important business of settling the oars comfortably in the rowlocks. Some weekend sailors, rich and poor, conceded Boller to himself, also threw their weight about because they knew what they were doing in a boat—but they were few and far between.

He didn't know for certain yet if his two passengers were sailors or not, although he already had his doubts about the younger man. Both men had distributed themselves carefully about the boat in a seaman-like manner and had actually managed not to rock the boat while clambering into it. They had even accomplished this without getting their feet wet, which was something of an achievement, and was connected, although his passengers did not know this, with the fact that Horace was sure of getting a handsome fee for the outing.

Doubtful payers and those who were so misguided as to attempt to undertip the boatman always got their feet wet.

The question of a fee for the journey they were about to undertake was very much on Detective Inspector Sloan's mind too. The payment—whatever it amounted to—would eventually have to come out of the Berebury Division imprest account. This was guarded by Superintendent Leeyes with a devotion to duty and tenacity of purpose that would have done credit to a Cerberus.

"Take you to where I found the poor man?" Horace nodded his comprehension. "That's what you want, isn't it?"

"It is," said Detective Inspector Sloan, detaching his mind with an effort from an unhappy vision of Superintendent Leeyes standing like a stag at bay over the petty cash at Berebury Police Station. "Can you do that for us?"

"Certainly, gentlemen," said Horace readily, even though he already knew that they were policemen not gentlemen; Horace's usage of modes of address was a nicely calculated affair and closely linked with the expectation of future reward. "No trouble at all."

Sloan settled himself at the bow of the boat, reminding himself that any hassle to come over payment for their trip should take second place to tangling with a murderer. He only hoped Superintendent Leeyes would feel the same.

For the fourth time that day the boatman began to row out into the estuary of the River Calle. Detective Inspector Sloan looked about him with interest. Seeing a map of the estuary with a cross marking the spot where the body had been found was one thing, but it was quite a different matter seeing the spot for oneself. He'd have to trust the boatman that it was the same spot though—he'd tried to rustle up Constable Ridgeford to get him to come with them, but according to Mrs. Ridgeford he'd had to go off on his bicycle to see to something. And so they had had to put to sea without him. Just, thought Sloan to himself, a distant memory stirring, the Owl and the Pussy-cat . . . except that Boller's old boat wasn't a beautiful pea-green . . .

Horace Boller had bent to the oars with practised ease and was rowing in a silence designed to save his breath. Then . . .

"You're going out to sea," observed Sloan sharply. "I thought you'd found him farther up river."

"Got to get round Billy's Finger, haven't I?" responded Boller resentfully.

"I see . . ." began Sloan.

"And pick up the tide." Nobody could be surlier than Boller when he wanted to be.

"Of course."

"I'm an old man now," said Boller, hunching his shoulders and allowing a whine to creep into his voice. "I can't go up river like I used to do."

"Naturally," said Sloan, crisply, nevertheless taking a good look at his watch. "Let me see now—what time was it exactly when we left?"

"I go by St. Peter's clock myself," snapped Boller. "Always keeps good time, does St. Peter's."

"Splendid," said Sloan warmly. "That'll make everything easier . . ." He settled back onto his hard seat. A warning shot fired across the bows never came amiss . . .

Presently the rowing boat did turn up river. Rowing against the eddies was not such hard work for Horace Boller as it would have been for most other men because he came of river people and knew every stretch of quiet water that there was. This did not stop him giving an artful pant as he eventually shipped his oars and caught a patch of slack water.

" 'Bout here it was, gentlemen," he said, histrionically drooping himself over the oars as if at the end of a fast trip from Putney to Mortlake against another crew.

Detective Inspector Sloan was concentrating on the water. "How far does the tide come up the estuary?"

The boatman wrinkled his eyes. "The sparling—they turn back half-way between Collerton and Edsway no matter what."

"They do, do they?" responded Sloan vigorously. The habits of sparling were no sort of an answer for a superintendent sitting at a desk in Berebury Police Station.

"Always go to the limit of the salt water, do sparling," said Boller.

"Ah," said Sloan. That was better. Sparling must be biological indicators too.

"Only see them in the summer, of course," said the boatman.

"Been this year then, have they?" asked Sloan, unconsciously lapsing into the vernacular himself.

"Not yet." Horace Boller unshipped an oar to stop the boat drifting too far.

"It's summer now," remarked Detective Constable Crosby from the stern.

"Not afore Collerton Fair," said Horace Boller flatly. "Sparling come at fair time."

Detective Inspector Sloan turned his head and regarded the southern shore of the river mouth with close attention. Not far away a heron rose and with an almost contemptuous idleness put the tips of his wing feathers out as spoilers. They'd left Edsway and the open sea well behind but they could now see Collerton Church clearly up river of them. Far inland were urban Berebury and ancient Calleford and what townspeople chose to call civilisation . . .

"Do smell of cucumber," rasped the boatman unexpectedly.

"What does?" asked Sloan. They were a long way from land.

"Sparling."

"Ah," said Sloan again, his mind on other things. "Pull the boat round a bit, will you? I want to see the other way."

The view down river was unrevealing. Edsway itself, though, was clearly visible, as was the headland beyond. Kinnisport and the cliffs at Cranberry Point were just a smudge in the distance.

"That headland behind Marby stands out, doesn't it?" observed Sloan, surprised. Seen from nearer to, the rise in the land wasn't quite so apparent.

"That's the Cat's Back," said Boller. "Proper seamark, that is."

"Funny," said Crosby ingenuously, "I never thought you had seamarks like you had landmarks."

Somewhere not very far away a gull screamed.

"Take us up river now," commanded Sloan abruptly.

Horace Boller bent to his oars once more. He rowed purposefully and without comment out of the narrowing estuary and into the river proper. Detective Inspector Sloan, sitting at the bow, was almost as immobile as a carved figurehead at the prow. He did turn once to begin to say something to Detective Constable Crosby, but that worthy officer was settled in the stern of the boat, letting his hand dangle in the water and regarding the consequent and subsequent wake with the close attention that should have been devoted to the duties of detection.

Sloan turned back and looked ahead. Speech would have been wasted. Instead he turned his mind to studying the river banks. That was when, presently, he too saw the doors of the boathouse belonging to Collerton House. Even from midstream he could see where a crowbar had been used to prise open the lock.

CHAPTER 11

This is a downright deep tragedy.

Frank Mundill was soon back at the riverside. This time he had Detective Inspector Sloan and Detective Constable Crosby with him, not Elizabeth Busby. Sloan had a distinct feeling that he had seen the man from Collerton House before but he couldn't immediately remember where.

Mundill indicated the boathouse doors very willingly to the two policemen and then pointed to the empty stretch of water inside the boathouse.

"Our dinghy's gone, Inspector," he said.

"And this, I take it, sir, is where she was kept, is it?" said Sloan, giving the inside of the boathouse a swift looking-over.

"It was." Mundill tightened his lips wryly. "She wasn't exactly the *Queen Elizabeth,* you know, but she was good enough for a day on the river with a rod."

Sloan examined the broken lock and loose hasp as best he could without getting his feet wet. There was a scar on the woodwork where something had rested to give leverage to a crowbar. Every picture told a story and this one seemed clear enough . . .

"Prised open all right, sir," he agreed presently. "Have you any idea when?"

Frank Mundill shook his head and explained that the damage would only have been visible from the path along the river bank and from the river itself. "I haven't been this way much myself recently, Inspector. My wife was ill from Easter onwards and I just didn't have the time." He gave a weary shrug of his shoulders. "And now that she's gone I haven't got the inclination."

Sloan pointed to the fishing rods on the boathouse wall. They looked quite valuable to him. "Are they all present and correct, sir?"

Mundill's face came up in a quick affirmative response, reinforcing Sloan's impression that he'd seen it before somewhere. "Oh, yes, Inspector. We think it's just the boat that's gone."

"We?" queried Sloan. The list of riparian owners had dealt in surnames. It hadn't gone into household detail.

"My late wife's niece is still with me. She came to nurse my wife and she's staying on until her parents get back from South America next week."

"I see, sir."

"She was out here with me earlier and we both agreed it was just *Tugboat Annie* that's gone."

Detective Inspector Sloan reached for his notebook in much the same way as Police Constable Brian Ridgeford had reached for his. A name put a different complexion on a police search for anything. A name on the unfortunate young man at Dr. Dabbe's forensic laboratory would be a great step forward. "*Tugboat Annie,* did you say, sir?"

"It won't help, I'm afraid, Inspector." Frank Mundill was apologetic. "That was just what we called her in the family."

The dead young man would have been called something in the family too. Sloan would have dearly liked to have known what it was.

"The name," expanded Frank Mundill, "wasn't actually written on her or anything like that."

"I see, sir," Sloan said, disappointed.

"She was only a fishing boat, you see, Inspector." He added, "And not a very modern fishing boat, at that. She was one of the relics of my father-in-law's day."

Sloan nodded, unsurprised. His own first impression had been of how very dated everything about Collerton House was. There was something very pre-Great War about the whole set-up—house, boathouse, grounds and all.

"I mustn't say, 'Those were the days,'" said Mundill drily,

waving an arm to encompass the boathouse and the fishing rods, "but I'm sure you know what I mean, Inspector."

"I do indeed, sir," agreed Sloan warmly. "Spacious, I think you could call them." As he had first entered Collerton House the stained glass of the inner front door and the wide sweep of the staircase had told him all he needed to know about the age of the house. It was Edwardian to a degree. Similarly the white polo-necked jersey of Frank Mundill had told him quite a lot about the man before him. He could have been a writer . . .

"Unfortunately," Mundill was saying, "the boathouse is very carefully screened from the house so I couldn't have seen anyone breaking in even though my studio faces north."

"An artist . . ." To his own surprise Sloan found he had said the words aloud.

"I'm an architect, Inspector," he said, adding astringently, "There are those of my professional brethren who would have said 'yes' to the word artist though."

"Well, sir, now that you come to mention it . . ."

"An architect is something of an artist certainly but he's something of an engineer too."

A policeman, thought Sloan, was something of a diplomat.

"As well as being a craftsman and a draughtsman, of course."

A policeman was something of a martinet, of course. He had to be.

"And, Inspector, if he's any good as an architect he's something of a visionary, too."

If a policeman was any good as a policeman he was something of a philosopher too. It didn't do not to be in the police force.

Mundill waved a tapered hand. "However . . ."

Then it came to Sloan where it was that he had seen the man's face before. "Your photograph was in the local paper last week, sir, wasn't it?"

The architect squinted modestly down his nose. "You saw it, Inspector, did you?"

"I did indeed," said Sloan handsomely. "The opening of the new fire station, wasn't it?"

"A very ordinary job, I'm afraid," said Mundill deprecatingly.

In the police force very ordinary jobs had a lot to be said for them. Out of the ordinary ones usually came up nasty.

"It is difficult," continued the architect easily, "to be other than strictly utilitarian when you're designing a hose tower."

"Quite so," said Sloan.

"We had site problems, of course," continued Frank Mundill smoothly, "it being right in the middle of the town."

Sloan nodded. Site problems would be to architects what identity problems were to the police, obstacles to be overcome.

"Mind you, Inspector, I have designed buildings in Berebury where there's been a little more scope than down at the fire station."

Municipal buildings being what they were Sloan was glad to hear it.

"There was the junior school," said Mundill.

"Split level," said Sloan, who had been there.

"Petty crime," added Crosby professionally. He had been there too.

"Plenty of site leeway in that case," said Mundill.

There was precious little leeway with an unknown body. Where did you start if "Missing Persons" didn't come up with anyone fitting the description of the body you had? The architect was warming to his theme. "There's more freedom with a school than there is with some domestic stuff."

Sloan looked up. "You do ordinary house plans, too, sir, do you?"

"Oh, yes, Inspector." He smiled thinly. "I do my share of the domestic side, all right."

All policemen did their share of the domestic side. "Domestics" were what new constables on the beat cut their wisdom teeth on. It aged them more quickly than anything else.

Sloan took a final look round the boathouse, and said formally, "I'll be in touch with you again, sir, about this break-in. In due course. Come along, Crosby . . ."

He turned to go but as he did so his ear caught the inimitable sound of the splash of oars. Sloan leaned out over the path and looked downstream as far as he could. He recognised Horace Boller and his boat quite easily. He had to screw up his eyes to see who his passenger was. And then he recognised him too. It was Mr. Basil Jensen, the curator of the Calleford Museum . . .

* * *

"Terry?" Miss Blandford pursed her lips. "Terry, did you say?"

"I did." Police Constable Brian Ridgeford had begun his search for a boy named Terry at the village school at Edsway. School was over for the day but the head teacher was still there. "Have you got any boys called Terry?"

"The trouble," said Miss Blandford, "is that we've got more than one."

"Tell me," invited Ridgeford, undaunted.

She opened the school register. "There's Terry Waters . . ."

"And what sort of a lad is Terry Waters?"

"Choirboy type," she said succinctly.

Ridgeford frowned.

"The 'butter wouldn't melt in his mouth' sort of boy," amplified the teacher.

Ridgeford's frown cleared.

She waved a hand. "If you know what I mean?"

Ridgeford knew what she meant. The manner of boy to whom benches of magistrates in juvenile courts—who should know better—almost automatically gave the benefit of the doubt . . .

"You probably passed him on your way here," said Miss Blandford. "He only lives down the road."

Ridgeford shook his head. "Not Terry Waters then."

He wasn't expecting Terry or his friend to be Edsway boys. Mrs. Boller would have recognised Edsway boys when they had brought the ship's bell into her shop. Children from all the other villages roundabout, though, came into Edsway school every day by bus. "What about the others?" he asked.

"There's Terry Wilkins."

Ridgeford got out his notebook. "Where does he hail from?"

"Collerton." She hesitated. "He's not a bad boy but easily led."

Ridgeford knew that sort. A boy who wouldn't take to crime unless the opportunity presented itself. There was a whole school of academic thought that saw crime as opportunity. Remove the opportunity, they said, and you removed the crime. If that didn't work you removed the criminal and called it preventive detention.

Miss Blandford said, "With Terry Wilkins it would depend on the temptation."

Constable Ridgeford nodded sagely. Who said Adam and Eve was nonsense? Temptation had had to begin somewhere. It didn't matter that it had only been an apple to begin with. It was the principle of the thing. "Go on," he said.

"There's Terry Goddard." The head teacher's face became as near to benign-looking as Ridgeford had seen it. "He's a worker."

"Ah."

"Not clever, mind you, but a worker."

Everyone liked a worker. Being a worker evidently exonerated Terry Goddard in Miss Blandford's eyes from any activity the police were likely to be mixed up in. Perhaps being a worker meant you weren't idle and that removed you a stage farther from temptation. Ridgeford tried to think of some industrious criminals.

Henri Landru must have been quite busy.

In the nature of things eleven murders took time.

Dr. Marcel Petiot couldn't have been much of a layabout either. He hadn't kept a stroke record of the murders he had committed but the French police thought sixty-five—give or take a few.

"That the lot, miss?" he said aloud. "I'd been hoping for someone from Marby."

"There's Terry Dykes." She looked Brian Ridgeford straight in the eye and said, "I don't know what you want your Terry for, Constable, but I wouldn't put anything past this one."

Ridgeford put the name down in his notebook. There was no

point in asking expert opinion if you didn't take account of it. He took down a Marby address with a certain amount of satisfaction, then he asked Miss Blandford if Terry Dykes had got a sidekick.

"I beg your pardon, Constable?"

Ridgeford searched in his mind for the right expression. "A best friend, miss." Bosom chum sounded distinctly old-fashioned but that was what he meant.

"Oh, yes." Her brow cleared. "Melvin Bates."

Ridgeford wrote that name down too.

"Melvin Bates hangs on Terry Dykes's every word, so," she gave a quick nod and said realistically, "I daresay that's two of them up to no good."

Police Constable Brian Ridgeford took his leave of the head teacher and applied himself to his bicycle and another journey to the fishing village beside the open sea. Judicious questioning of Marby natives led the policeman to the harbour. He'd find his quarry there for sure, he was told. They were always there, messing about in boats. Or just messing about. But as sure as eggs they'd be there.

So they were.

Two boys.

There had been something that Brian Ridgeford dimly remembered in his training that advised against the questioning of juveniles by a police officer in uniform. Because of the neighbours. Brian Ridgeford squared his shoulders. There weren't any neighbours on the eastern arm of the harbour wall.

Just two boys.

They saw him coming and at the same time saw that there was no point in retreating. They stood their ground as he approached, one standing against a capstan and the other with one foot on a coil of rope.

"About that ship's bell," began Ridgeford generally.

"Wasn't worth nothing," said the boy by the capstan.

"The old woman said so," chimed in the other.

"Load of old iron," said the first boy, kicking the capstan with his foot.

"Waste of time going over there," said his friend.

"She wouldn't give us nothing for it," said the boy who was kicking the capstan. "You ask her."

"Where did you get it?" asked Ridgeford.

"Up on the Cat's Back," replied the first boy glibly. "Didn't we, Mel?"

"Up on the Cat's Back," agreed Melvin. "Like Terry said."

"Did you now?" said Ridgeford evenly. "Suppose you tell me exactly where."

"By an old tree," said Terry.

"Near the hut," said Melvin at the same time.

"By an old tree near the hut," said Terry promptly.

Constable Ridgeford decided that Terry Dykes already had the makings of a criminal mentality.

"I suppose," said the policeman heavily, "that it fell off the back of a lorry up there."

"No," began Melvin, "it was in . . ."

"There's only a footpath," Terry Dykes cut in quickly.

Any resemblance to the tableau formed by the three of them to Sir John Millais's famous painting "The Boyhood of Raleigh" was purely coincidental. True, there was more than one beached rowing boat on the shore in the background and there were certainly two boys and an adult in the composition but there any likeness ended. In Millais's picture the two boys had been hanging, rapt, on the words of the ancient mariner as he pointed out to sea and described the wonders he had seen. In the present instance the tales were being told by the boys and Brian Ridgeford wasn't pointing anywhere. He was, however, projecting extreme scepticism at what he heard.

"So it didn't fall off the back of a lorry then," he said.

"No," said Terry Dykes defensively, "it didn't."

"Just lying there then, was it?"

"Yes . . . No . . . I don't know."

"You must know."

Terry Dykes shut his lips together.

"Make up your mind, boy," said Ridgeford not unkindly. "Was it or wasn't it?"

"No," said Terry sullenly, "it wasn't just lying there."

"Well, then, where was it?" demanded Ridgeford. When there was no reply from Dykes he suddenly swung round on Melvin Bates. "All right, you tell me."

Melvin Bates started to stutter. "I . . . I . . . it was in . . ."

"Shut up," said Dykes, unceremoniously cutting off his henchman.

"All right," said Ridgeford flatly, "I've got the message. The bell was inside somewhere, wasn't it?" He drew breath. "Now then, let me see if I can work out where. Over here in Marby?" They were known as "constraint questions"; those whose answers limited the area of doubt. The best-known constraint question was "Can you eat it?" Ridgeford allowed his voice to grow a harder note. "And you found it inside somewhere, didn't you?"

It took him another ten minutes to find out exactly where.

* * *

Constable Ridgeford was not the only policeman whose immediate quarry lay in Marby. As soon as Sloan and Crosby left Collerton House they too made for the fishing village by the sea.

"We'll pick up Ridgeford over there," predicted Sloan, "and he can take us to have a look at this dinghy he's reported."

They'd left Basil Jensen still making his way upstream.

"To see if it's *Tugboat Annie,*" completed Crosby, engaging gear.

"It would figure if it were." He paused and then said quietly, "I think something else figures, too, Crosby."

"Sir?"

"I think—only think, mind you—that we just may have an explanation for a body decomposed but not damaged."

"Sir?"

"You think, too," adjured Sloan. The road between Collerton and Marby was so rural that not even Crosby could speed on it. He could use his mind instead.

"The boathouse?" offered the detective constable uncertainly.

"The boathouse," said Sloan with satisfaction. "It's early

days yet, Crosby, but I think that we shall find that our chap—whoever he is—was parked in the water in the boathouse after he was killed."

"Why in the water, though, sir?"

"The answer to that," said Sloan briskly, "is something called mephitis."

"Sir?"

"Mephitis," spelled out Sloan for him, "is the smell of the dead."

Crosby assimilated this and then said, "So he was killed by a fall from a height first somewhere else . . ."

"Somewhere else," agreed Sloan at once.

"But . . ."

"But left in the water afterwards, Crosby."

"Why?"

Sloan waved a hand. "As I said before graves for murder victims don't come easy."

"Yes, sir," Crosby nodded. "Besides, he might have been killed on the spur of the moment and whoever did it needed time to think what to do with the body."

It was surprising how the word "murderer" hung outside speech.

"He might," agreed Sloan. He hoped that it had been a hot-blooded affair. Murder had nothing to be said for it at any time but heat-of-the-moment murder was always less sinister than murder plotted and planned. "He would need time and opportunity to work out what to do."

"And then," postulated Crosby, "the body was just pushed out into the water?"

There is a tide in the affairs of men, which, taken at the flood, leads on . . . No, that wouldn't do. It wouldn't have been like that at all. It would have been the furtive opening of the boathouse doors during the hours of darkness, and after the furtive opening the silent shove of a dead body with a boat-hook while the River Calle searched out every cranny of the river bank and picked up its latest burden and bore it off towards the sea.

"Unless I'm very much mistaken," said Sloan austerely, "the body left the boathouse at night."

"Yes, sir."

"Probably," he added, "in time to catch an ebb-tide." He, Sloan, would have to look at a tide table as soon as he got back to the police station but darkness and an ebb-tide made sense.

"Do we know when, sir?" asked Crosby, who was perforce driving at a speed to satisfy his passenger.

"Some time before he was found," said Sloan dourly, "but not too long before."

That was a lay interpretation of what Dr. Dabbe had said in longer words.

Long enough to pick up *gammarus pulex.*

Long enough to become unrecognisable.

Long enough to be taken by the river to the sea.

Not so long as to be taken by that same sea and laid on Billy's Finger.

Not so long as to disintegrate completely.

That would have been something that an assassin might have hoped for, that the body would fall to pieces.

Or that it would reach the open sea and be seen no more . . .

"Why did the boat go too?" Crosby was enquiring.

"I think," reasoned Sloan aloud, "that if a boat is found adrift and a body is found in the water simple policemen are meant to put two and two together and make five."

That was something else a murderer might have hoped for.

"It might have happened too," said Crosby, "mightn't it? He'd only got to get a bit farther out to sea and he wouldn't have been spotted at all."

Sloan stared unseeingly out of the car window. "I wonder why he was put into the river exactly when he was."

On such a full sea are we now afloat . . .

"Well, you wouldn't choose a weekend, would you, sir?" said Crosby.

Never on Sunday?

"The whole estuary's stuffed with sailing boats at the week-end," continued the constable. "You should see it, sir."

"I probably will," said Sloan pessimistically, "unless we've got all this cleared up by then."

The detective constable slowed down for a signpost. "This must be the Edsway to Marby road we're joining."

"Something," said Sloan resolutely, "must have made it important for that body to be got out of that boathouse when it was."

The car radio began to chatter while he was speaking. "The gentlemen from the press," reported the girl at the microphone, "would like to know when Detective Inspector Sloan will see them."

"Ten o'clock tomorrow morning," responded Sloan with spirit, "and not a minute before." He switched off at his end and turned to his companion. "And Crosby . . ."

"Sir?"

"While you're about it," said Sloan, "you'd better find out about the niece. And what Mrs. Mundill died from too. We can't be too careful."

"Yes, sir."

"Now, where did Ridgeford say this dinghy was?"

"According to his report," said Crosby, "it's beyond the Marby lifeboat station. To be exact, to the north of it. We're to ask for a man called Farebrother."

CHAPTER 12

But hark! I hear the toll of a bell.

Farebrother was quite happy to indicate the stray dinghy to the two policemen. And to tell them that Ridgeford was down on the harbour wall.

"Fetch him," said Sloan briefly to Crosby. He turned to Farebrother and showed him the copper barbary head. "Ever seen one of these before?"

"Might have," said the lifeboatman. "Might not."

"Lately?"

"Might have," said the lifeboatman again.

"How lately?"

"I don't hold with such things," he said flatly.

"No," said Sloan.

" 'Tisn't right to disturb places where men lie." Farebrother stared out to sea.

Sloan said nothing.

"Mark my words," said Farebrother, "no good comes of it."

Sloan nodded.

" 'Tisn't lucky either."

"Unlucky for some, anyway," said Sloan obliquely, bingo-style.

"Didn't ought to be allowed, that's what I say."

"Quite so," said Sloan.

"They say there was the bones of a man's hand still clutching a candlestick down there."

"Down where?" said Sloan softly.

Farebrother's mouth set in an obstinate line. "I don't know where. No matter who asks me, be they as clever as you like."

"Who asked you?"

"Never you mind that. I tell you I don't know anything . . ."

"Neither do I," said Sloan seriously, "but I intend to find out."

"That's your business," said Farebrother ungraciously, "but I say things should be let alone with, that's what I say." He turned on his heel and crunched off over the shingle.

Crosby came back with Ridgeford while Sloan was still examining the old fishing boat. Sloan pointed to Farebrother's retreating back. *"The Old Man and the Sea,"* he said neatly to the two constables. They both looked blank. He changed his tone. "This bell, Ridgeford . . ."

"Taken, sir, from a farm up on the Cat's Back," said Ridgeford. "Or so the two boys who took it into Mother Hopton's say. I don't think they were having me on but you never can tell." Ridgeford had learned some things already. "Not with boys."

"Not with boys," agreed Sloan.

"The farmer's called Manton," said Ridgeford. "Alec Manton of Lea Farm."

"Do you know him?"

Ridgeford shook his head. "Not to say know. I've heard of him, that's all, sir."

"Heard what?"

"Nothing against."

Sloan nodded. "Right, then you can stay in the background. Crosby, you're coming with me to Manton's farm. Now, Ridgeford, whereabouts exactly did you say this sheep fank was that the boys told you about?"

Few farmers can have been fortunate enough to see as much of their farm laid out in front of them as did Alec Manton. The rising headland was almost entirely given over to sheep and the fields were patterned with the casual regularity of patchwork. Because of the rise in the land the farmland and its stock were both easily visible. The farmhouse, though, was nestled into the low ground before the headland proper began, sheltered alike from sea and wind. It was in the process of being restored and extended. Sloan noticed a discreet grey and white board proclaiming that Frank Mundill was the architect, and made a note.

Alec Manton was out, his wife told them. She was a plump, calm woman, undismayed by the presence of two police officers at the farm. Was it about warble fly?

"Not exactly," temporised Sloan, explaining that he would nevertheless like to look at the sheep-fold on the hill.

"Where they dip?" said Mrs. Manton intelligently. "Of course. You go on up and I'll tell my husband to come along when he comes home. He shouldn't be long."

In the event they didn't get as far as the sheep fank before the farmer himself caught up with them.

"Routine investigations," said Sloan mendaciously.

"Oh?" said Manton warily. He was tallish with brown hair.

"We've had a report that something might have been stolen from the farm."

"Have you?" said Alec Manton. He was a man who looked as if he packed a lot of energy. He looked Sloan up and down. "Can't say that we've missed anything."

"No?" said Sloan.

"What sort of thing?"

"A ship's bell."

"From my farm?" Alec Manton's face was quite expressionless.

"Boys," said Sloan sedulously. "They said it came from where you keep your sheep."

"Did they?" said Manton tightly. "Then we'd better go and see, hadn't we? This way . . ."

Their goal was several fields away, set in a faint hollow in the land, and built against the wind. In front of the little bothy was a sheep-dipping tank. Set between crush pen and drafting pen, it was full of murky water. Alec Manton led the way into the windowless building and looked round in the semidarkness. Sloan and Crosby followed on his heels. There was nothing to see save bare walls and even barer earth. The place, though, did show every sign of having been occupied by sheep at some time. Sloan looked carefully at the floor. It had been pounded by countless hooves to the consistency of concrete.

"This bell," began Sloan.

"That you say was found . . ." said Manton.

"In police possession," said Sloan mildly.

"Ah."

"Pending enquiries."

"I see."

"Of course," said Sloan largely, "the boys may have been having us on."

"Of course."

"You know what boys are."

"Only too well," said Manton heartily.

"We'll have to get on to them again," said Sloan, "and see if we can get any nearer the truth, whatever that may be."

"Of course," said the farmer quickly. "Did they—er—take anything else, do you know?"

"Not that we know about," said Sloan blandly. "Would there have been anything else in there for them to steal?"

Alec Manton waved an arm. "You've seen it for yourself, haven't you? Give or take a sheep or two from time to time it looks pretty empty to me."

"Of course," said Sloan casually, "the owner of this bell may turn up to claim it."

"That would certainly simplify matters," agreed the farmer. "But in the meantime . . ."

"Yes, sir?"

"It's quite safe in police custody?"

"Quite safe," Sloan assured him.

* * *

"Crosby!" barked Sloan.

"Sir?"

"What was odd about all that?"

"Don't know, sir."

"Think, man. Think."

"The place was empty."

"Of course it was empty," said Sloan with asperity. "The bell must have been tucked away in the corner when those two boys found it. Only boys would have looked there . . ."

Murderers who thought that they had hidden their victims well reckoned without the natural curiosity of the average boy at their peril. Many a well-covered thicket had been penetrated by a boy for no good reason . . .

"Yes, sir," said Crosby.

"What wasn't empty, Crosby?"

Crosby thought for a long moment. "Sir?"

"What was full, Crosby?"

"Only the sheep-dipping thing."

"Exactly," breathed Sloan. "Do you know what month it is, Crosby?"

"June, sir," said Crosby stolidly.

"You don't," said Sloan softly, "dip sheep in Calleshire in June."

"Left over from when you did, then," suggested Crosby.

"No," said Sloan.

"No?"

"You dip sheep a month after shearing. Manton's sheep weren't shorn," said Sloan. Policemen, even town policemen, knew all about the dipping of sheep and its regulations. "Besides, you wouldn't leave your sheep-dip full without a good reason. It's dangerous stuff."

"What sort of reason?" said Crosby.

"If," said Sloan, "you have been conducting a secret rescue of the parts of an old East Indiaman you acquire items which have been underwater for years."

"Yes, sir."

"Taking them out of the water causes them to dry up and disintegrate. Mr. Jensen at the museum said so."

"Yes, sir, I'm sure."

"So you have to store them underwater or else."

"Yes, sir."

"Wooden things, that is."

Crosby nodded, not very interested. "Wooden things."

"Metal ones," said Sloan, "aren't so important."

"What about rust?"

"Bronze doesn't rust," said Sloan.

"*The Clarembald*'s bell?"

"Bronze," said Sloan. "Or so Ridgeford said."

"It didn't need to stay underwater?"

"No," said Sloan. "It could stand in the corner of the sheep building quite safely." He amended this. "Safe from everything except boys." He drew breath and carried on. "There was another thing about what was in that sheep-dipping tank."

"Sir?"

"Think, Crosby."

"It was dirty, sir. You couldn't see if there was anything in there or not."

"That and something else," said Sloan, and waited.

Dull, a constable.

That had been in Shakespeare.

He'd thought of everything, had the bard.

The detective inspector cleared his throat and said didactically, "A good policeman uses all his senses."

Crosby lifted his nose like a pointer. "But it didn't smell, sir."

"Precisely," said Sloan grimly. "Like the dog that didn't bark in the night, it didn't smell. Believe you me, lad, sheep-dip isn't by any manner of means the most fragrant of fluids."

"No, sir."

"But I'm prepared to bet that there was something in that tank besides dirty water."

Crosby scuffed his toe at a pebble. "I still don't see what it's got to do with the body in the water."

"Neither do I, Crosby, neither do I. What I wonder is if Mr. Basil Jensen does."

* * *

Elizabeth Busby just couldn't settle. She was like a bee working over a flower-bed already sucked dry of all its nectar. She couldn't settle to anything at all, not to finishing off spring-cleaning the spare bedroom and not to any other household chores either.

She met Frank Mundill in the hall as he came back from the boathouse. He dropped the key back into the drawer in the hall table.

"I don't know why I bothered to lock it, I'm sure," he said. "Anyone who wanted to could get into the boathouse as easy as wink."

"Tea?" she suggested.

"That would be nice." He looked unenthusiastically at the flight of stairs that led up to his studio. "I don't think I'll go back to the drawing board this minute."

"No," she agreed with the sentiment as well as the statement. Getting on with anything just now was difficult enough. Going back to something was quite impossible.

Presently Mundill said, "I'll have to go along and have a word with Ted Boller about getting the river doors fixed up."

She nodded.

"It'll have to be something temporary." He grimaced. "The police want the damage left."

"Evidence, I suppose," she said without interest.

"They're sending a photographer."

"I'll keep my ears open," she promised. She would hear the bell all right when they came. She had always heard her aunt's bell and her ear was still subconsciously attuned to listening for it. At the first tinkle she'd been awake and on her way to the bedroom . . .

"I may be a little while," said Mundill, elaborately casual.

She looked up, her train of thought broken.

"While I'm about it," he said, "I might as well go on down to Veronica Feckler's cottage and see exactly what it is that she wants doing there."

"Might as well," agreed Elizabeth in a desultory fashion.

"You might keep your ear open for the telephone . . ."

She nodded. His secretary was going to be away all the week. "I will. There might be a call for me too."

"Of course," he agreed quickly.

Too quickly.

She'd practically lived on the telephone while Peter Hinton was around. When he wasn't at Collerton House he was at the College of Technology at Luston. His landlady—well versed in student ways—had a pay telephone in the hall. Peter Hinton had spent a great deal of time on it. Elizabeth's eyes drifted involuntarily to the instrument in the hall of Collerton House. It was by a window-seat and Elizabeth had spent a similar amount of time curled up on that window-seat enjoying those endless chats. Politicians and business negotiators had a phrase which covered young lovers as well. They often began either their alliances or their confrontations with what they called "exploratory talks."

So it had been with Elizabeth Busby and Peter Hinton. Their talks had been exploratory too, as they each searched out the recesses of mind and memory of the other, revealing—as the politicians and businessmen found to their cost—a little of themselves too in the process. In some ways these preliminaries of a courtship had been like playing that old pencil-and-paper parlour game of Battleships. Sometimes a tentative salvo fell in a square that represented the empty sea. Sometimes it fell where the opponent's battleship was placed and then there was a hit—a palpable hit. After that it was an easy matter to find and sink the paper battleship and win the game.

So it was with young people getting to know each other.

One thing they found they had in common was parents abroad. His were tea planters in Assam.

What they didn't share was an interest in crime. Peter Hinton knew most of the Notable British Trials series of books by heart and took an interest in villainy. Elizabeth shied away from the unpleasant like a nervous horse.

And then suddenly she'd found she hadn't known Peter Hinton at all . . .

Exploratory talks didn't always lead on to treaties and alliances. Sometimes—the news bulletins said so—they broke down, foundering upon this or that rock uncovered in the course of those very talks. So it must have been with Peter Hinton. Only she didn't know what it was that had been laid bare that had been such a stumbling block between the two of them that they couldn't even discuss it. He'd come into her life out of the blue and as precipitately he'd gone out of it again.

She brought the tea tray back into the hall for them both. There was a little occasional table there and Frank Mundill pulled it over to the window-seat. The only trouble with being in the window-seat was that whoever was sitting there could not avoid the full impact of the picture hanging on the wall opposite. It had been quite one of Richard Camming's most ambitious paintings.

"We think," Celia Mundill used to say to visitors to the house seeing it for the first time, "that it's meant to be Diana the Huntress."

"But we never liked to ask," Marion Busby would add tremulously if she were there.

"Up to something, of course."

"But we don't quite know what."

They had both been fond of their father but they had loved him without illusion.

Elizabeth was able to pour out the tea without thinking about Diana the Huntress. As always when she was sitting in the hall her eyes drifted to the model of the Camming valve. It was the Camming valve on which the family fortunes had been founded. It was the Camming valve which had brought Peter Hinton into her life. He'd come from Luston College of Technology with a dissertation to do. He'd chosen the Camming valve and its influence on the development of the marine engine. What more natural that he should come to Gordon Camming's house in the course of writing it? True, Gordon Camming had actually designed his valve in the back kitchen of some Victorian artisan's cottage, demolished long ago in a vigorous council slum clearance scheme, but Collerton House was what he had built. It was a monument to his success and as near to a museum as there was.

Frank Mundill had sunk his tea with celerity. "I'll be going now," he said, getting to his feet.

She nodded, her train of thought scarcely disturbed this time. In her mind's eye she was seeing Peter Hinton bending over the model as he had done the first day he came.

"We've got a drawing of it at the college," he said when he saw it, "but not a model."

"It's a working model," she had said eagerly, anxious to be helpful. "Grandfather used to make it work for me when I was little. I can't do it, though."

He had come . . .

She remembered now his tiny smile as he had said, "I can. Would you like to see it working again?"

He had seen . . .

"Oh, please."

He had conquered . . .

He'd come back again, of course, another day. And another day. And another.

What she couldn't understand was why he had gone and not come back.

She sat in the window-seat now, taking her tea in thoughtful sips. She sat there so long that the cushion became less comfortable. She shifted her position slightly, almost without thinking. To her surprise this made for less comfort rather than more. Something was sticking into her. The fact took a moment or two to penetrate her consciousness. When it did she put her hand down between the cushions. It encountered something oblong and unyielding. She stood up abruptly and snatched the cushions away. All doubt ended when she set eyes on the object.

It was Peter Hinton's slide rule and she knew it well.

OFFICIALLY NOTED

CHAPTER 13

'Tis what we must all come to.

Some savage breasts cannot be soothed. That of Superintendent Leeyes came into this category.

"What I want, Sloan," he snapped, "are results."

Detective Inspector Sloan was reporting to him in the superintendent's office at Berebury. "Yes, sir, but . . ."

"Not theories."

"No, sir." Actually Sloan didn't have any theories either but this seemed to have escaped the superintendent's notice.

"Have you any idea at all what's going on over there?"

"Finding *The Clarembald* comes into it," said Sloan slowly, "though where the dead man fits in with that I really don't know."

"Don't forget that he had that copper thing . . ."

"Barbary head."

"In his pocket."

"Yes, sir, so he did." Sloan cleared his throat. "But there are a lot of other things we don't know."

"Who he is," trumpeted Leeyes. "You haven't got very far with that, have you, Sloan?"

"We have one lead, sir. The girl at Collerton House had a boy-friend who's not around any more. Crosby's chasing him up now just to be on the safe side."

"There's another thing we don't know besides who the body is."

"Why he was set out into the mainstream when he was," said Sloan before the superintendent could say it for him.

"Exactly," growled Leeyes.

This was one of the things that was puzzling Sloan too. "There must have been a reason," he agreed. "After all he'd been dead for quite a while and in the water too. Dr. Dabbe said so."

"And then suddenly someone . . ."

"The murderer," said Sloan. That was something he felt sure about.

"The murderer decides to punt him into the river."

"There'll be a reason," said Sloan confidently. "We're dealing with someone with brains."

Leeyes grunted again.

"Anyone," said Sloan feelingly, "who can kill someone without them being reported missing has got brains."

"It doesn't happen often," conceded Leeyes.

"And anyone who can find somewhere as clever as a boathouse to park a body until it's unrecognisable knows what they're doing. Do you realise, sir," he added energetically, "that if that man Horace Boller hadn't been out there fishing that body might well have just drifted out to sea and never been seen again?"

"A perfect murder," commented Leeyes.

"Exactly, sir." Though for the life of him Sloan didn't know why murder done and not known about should be called perfect . . .

"The dinghy," said Leeyes. "What about the dinghy?"

"I think that went just in case the body was picked up," said Sloan.

"A touch of local colour, eh?" said Leeyes grimly.

"We've examined it," said Sloan, "and it answers to Mr. Mundill's description. I don't think there's any doubt that it's the one from his boathouse but we'll get him over in the morning to identify it properly."

"That's all very well, Sloan, but where does *The Clarembald* come in?"

"I don't know, sir. The things from the ship," he couldn't bring himself to use the word "artefacts" to the superintendent, "that have been coming ashore . . ."

"Treasure trove," said Leeyes, never one to split hairs on precise meanings.

"Perhaps, sir. I don't know about that yet."

"These things then . . ." said Leeyes impatiently.

"Indicate that someone has found the East Indiaman."

"Don't forget the diver, eh, Sloan, don't forget the diver."

"No, sir, I haven't. This farmer—Alec Manton—has been hiring a local trawler. Ridgeford saw it going out at low tide."

"Did he indeed?" There was a pause while Superintendent Leeyes considered this and then he abruptly started on quite a different tack. "This height that Dr. Dabbe says he fell from . . ."

"I've been thinking about that, sir," said Sloan. Every case was like solving a jigsaw and some pieces of that jigsaw had straight edges. A piece of jigsaw puzzle that had a straight edge helped to define the puzzle. So it was in a murder case. He always thought of the forensic pathologist's report as so many pieces of straight edge of a jigsaw puzzle. And the pathologist had said that the man had fallen to his death. That became fact . . .

"Well?"

"Apart from the cliffs . . ."

"Which are too high."

"There isn't very much in the way of a drop round Collerton and Edsway." Inland from the cliffs the rest of the Calleshire littoral was—like Norfolk—very flat.

"He fell from somewhere," said Leeyes, who had taken Dr. Dabbe's report for gospel too.

"A dying fall," said Sloan, conscious that it had been said before.

"But where from?" asked Leeyes irritably. "Would a church tower have done?"

"It's the right sort of height," agreed Sloan, "but it's not exactly what you could call private, is it, sir? I mean, would you climb a church tower after dark with a murderer?"

"No," said Leeyes robustly. "And I wouldn't buy a second-hand car from one either."

"I'll get Crosby to check at Collerton Church anyway," said

Sloan, "but what I think we're looking for is a sort of hidden drop. Remember he would have had to have been pushed from the top and then stayed at the bottom . . ."

"Dead or dying."

"Until whoever pushed him came down and picked up the body."

"Darkness or privacy," agreed Leeyes.

What was it that Crosby had said?

Pussy's down the well.

It would have had to have been somewhere where murderer and victim could have gone together without comment.

Then the lonely push . . .

"And," said Leeyes, "then the body had to be got from wherever it fell to the boathouse. Have you gone into the logistics, Sloan?"

"The boot of a car would have done."

"And then?"

"For the last part? A wheelbarrow," said Sloan. "That would have done too. It's the easiest way to carry a body that I know. And there are several around the house."

"Not one of these plastic affairs, Sloan. You mean a good old-fashioned metal one."

"Yes, sir." When a man came automatically to put the word "good" together with the word "old-fashioned," it was time for him to retire. He coughed. "The trouble, sir, is that there is a perfectly good asphalt path to the boathouse that doesn't show any extra marks. We've looked."

Leeyes grunted. "So what you're saying is that he could have been killed anywhere and brought to Collerton."

"By land or water," said Sloan flatly. "With a barbary head in his pocket." That barbary head was a puzzle. Was it a pointer to *The Clarembald* or was it to point them away from someone else?

"It's what you might call wide open still, isn't it, Sloan," said Leeyes unencouragingly. "You'll have to look on it as a challenge," he added.

"I'm starting with a search warrant for Lea Farm at Marby," said Sloan flatly. "There's something funny going on there."

* * *

Landladies didn't always come up middle-aged and inquisitive. Sometimes they were young and indifferent.

"Pete?" said Ms. Cheryl Watson, shrugging her shoulders. "He was around."

"When?" asked Detective Constable Crosby.

She opened her hands expressively. "Don't ask me. He'll be back."

"When?" asked Crosby.

"When he feels like it. He'll settle up for his room all right, don't worry."

Crosby did not say that that was not what was worrying the county constabulary.

"What about his gear?" he said instead.

"Still around," she said largely. "And his mail. He'll be back for them."

"Why did he go?"

Her eyes opened wide. "He had exams, didn't he?"

"You think he chickened out?"

"A man has to be himself," said the self-appointed representative of a different way of life, "hasn't he?"

"I wouldn't know about that," said Crosby.

"Examinations are the sign of a decadent culture," pronounced the young woman. "Always making you prove yourself."

"A sort of initiation rite, you mean?" suggested Crosby.

"That's right," she said eagerly.

The course at the Police Training College made a man prove himself. Or leave. It was a sort of initiation rite too. A police constable was let into the mysteries of the service at the same time as he was being sorely tried by his instructors.

Ms. Watson looked Detective Constable Crosby up and down with unattractive shrewdness. "Is Pete in trouble then?"

"Not that we know about," said Crosby truthfully.

"There was something else besides examinations."

"Was there?" he murmured.

"He had a bird."

"Ah."

"Don't say that." She looked at him. "No, Pete was hell-bent on marriage."

"Was he?"

"No less," she said. "He was real old-fashioned about it."

Crosby gave the absent Mr. Hinton a passing thought.

"He often said he wasn't going to settle for anything less than marriage."

"Makes a change," said Crosby. The beat made a man philosophical about some things.

"She'd got money, you see," said Ms. Watson simply. "Or would have one day. I think that's what he said."

It is a truth universally acknowledged that a single man seeking good fortune must be in want of a wife in possession of one . . .

"Anyway," she said, "don't you worry. Pete Hinton is old enough to take care of himself."

Crosby said he was sure he hoped so too, but he came away with a disturbing description.

* * *

Elizabeth Busby sat alone in the empty house. She sat quite still at one end of the window-seat staring at that which she had found at the other.

Peter Hinton's slide rule.

It must have slipped out of his pocket the last time he had sat there. It couldn't have been before that because he would have missed it and then—for sure—a search on a grand scale would have been instituted. If it hadn't been found, then St. Anthony's aid would have been invoked. A practical young man like Peter Hinton hadn't really believed in St. Anthony, but Elizabeth had done so, and gradually Peter Hinton had begun to call upon him too for lost things.

Or said he had done.

His precious slide rule would have been missed very early

on. It was never out of his pocket—it was almost his badge of office. His course at Luston was a sandwich affair—so much time at his studies, so much time on the shop floor. His shop floor employment had been with Punnett and Punnett, Marine Engineers, Ltd., and it was after that when he went to the College of Technology. And much as very young doctors flaunted their stethoscopes, so the slide rules of embryo engineers were frequently in evidence.

She cast her mind back yet again to his last visit. In fact she had already gone over it in her mind a hundred times or more—searching every recollection for pointers of what was to come. She hadn't found any—their only disagreement had been about her aunt—and now she couldn't recollect either any indication that the famous slide rule hadn't been around. She screwed up her eyes in concentrated memory recall and came up with something that surprised her. Surely they hadn't been near the window-seat on Peter's last visit at all?

He'd come over from Luston to see her—it had had to be like that since Celia Mundill had begun to be so ill after Easter—on one of her aunt's really bad days. Elizabeth had been dividing her time between the bedroom and the kitchen. There had been no spare time for sitting together on the window-seat or anywhere else. In fact she hadn't had a great deal of time to spare for Peter Hinton at all but that had been simply because of her aunt's illness. She had wondered for a moment if it had been this which had so miffed him that he had taken his departure, but what manner of man would begrudge her time spent with the dying?

Because her aunt had been dying. Elizabeth had known that ever since Celia's X-ray at Easter when Frank Mundill had taken her to one side and told her that that was what the doctor over at Calleford had said. He'd brought a letter back with him for Dr. Tebot, Celia Mundill's own doctor at Collerton—dear old Dr. Tebot who looked like nothing so much as the doctor in Luke Fildes's famous picture—but he had enjoined secrecy on Dr. Tebot as well as on Elizabeth. Celia Mundill had an inoperable cancer of the stomach but she wasn't to know.

"Not ever," Frank Mundill had said at the time.

"But the doctor . . ."

"The doctor," said Mundill, "said she need never know."

"I don't see how."

"They call it 'stealing death,'" Frank Mundill had told her.

Come away, come away, death . . .

"Dr. Tebot said it's not as difficult as it sounds, Elizabeth, because the patient always wants to believe that they're getting better."

"A sort of conspiracy," Elizabeth remembered saying slowly at the time.

"A conspiracy of silence," Mundill had said firmly. "You don't need to lie. Anyway, Elizabeth, she won't ask you."

"No . . ."

"She'll ask the doctor and he'll know what to say, I'm sure."

"I'm sure, too," she'd said then with a touch of cynicism beyond her years.

And she had proceeded to watch her aunt decline. Severe vomiting had been accompanied by loss of weight. Abdominal pain had come, too, until the doctor had stopped it with a hefty pain-killer. It had needed injections though to stop the pains in her arms and legs. The district nurse had come to give her those and Elizabeth had been glad of the extra support.

Nothing though had stopped the vomiting or the burning pain in the patient's throat.

Or her loss of weight.

Frank Mundill had been marvellously attentive. At any moment of the night or day when Celia had said she could eat or drink he'd been on hand with something. Gradually though she'd sunk beyond that.

"She may get jaundiced," Dr. Tebot had warned them one day.

So she had. Soon after that her skin took on a yellow, jaundiced look. Celia Mundill had died too with the brown petechiae of premature age on her skin. One day she'd slipped into a merciful coma.

That, when it happened, though, was too late for Peter Hinton. He'd taken himself off by the time Celia Mundill had breathed her last. Perhaps, Elizabeth had thought more than once, he couldn't stand the atmosphere of illness—there were some men, she knew, who couldn't. Thank goodness Frank Mundill hadn't been one of them or she would never have coped. He'd been marvellous.

She sat quite still now in the window-seat, increasingly confident that the last time that Peter Hinton had come to the house they had not sat together there. They'd only met in the kitchen. Elizabeth had been waiting and watching for the district nurse while Frank Mundill was taking his turn in the bedroom beside the patient. She remembered now how difficult she had found it to think or speak of anything but her aunt's illness.

True, they'd nearly quarrelled but not about themselves.

About Celia Mundill.

"She looks so awful now," Elizabeth had cried. That had been the worst thing of all. Celia Mundill was just a ghastly parody of the woman she had been a few short months ago.

"What about her going into hospital?" Peter had urged. "Don't you think she ought to be in hospital? I do."

"No!" She'd been surprised at her own fierceness. She must have caught it from Frank Mundill. "We want her to die at home in her own bed. Besides," she said illogically, "she's far too poorly to go into hospital."

"Do her eyes water?" asked Peter suddenly.

"Yes, they do. Why?"

"I just wondered."

"There's nothing more they could do for her if she was in hospital," said Elizabeth, still het up over his suggestion. "We're doing all anybody could. Dr. Tebot says so."

"I'm sure you are," he said soothingly. "It was only a thought. But don't you go and knock yourself up, will you?"

"I'm young and strong," she had said, and she meant it.

Now—since Peter had gone and her aunt had died—she wasn't sure how strong she was. She wasn't as young as she had been either.

She stared at the slide rule.

It hadn't been missing that last evening that Peter Hinton

had come. She was certain about that. He would undoubtedly have mentioned the fact and gone hunting for his instrument. And he hadn't lost it that evening because they hadn't sat in the hall at all.

She shivered involuntarily.

That only left the time that he had come over—the time which she had never been able to fathom—when he had left the note and the ring on the hall table. In spite of herself her eyes drifted over in the direction of the hall table, seeing in her mind's eye the piece of paper and the circlet of metal lying there again—just as she had done the first time. She'd been carrying her aunt's tray down the stairs at the time . . .

She looked round the hallway. Surely he wouldn't have sat on the window-seat to compose the note? *Congés* deserved to have more time spent on them than that. Besides she might have come down the stairs at any time and found him sitting there and that would never have done. She rejected the notion almost as soon as she had thought of it. No, that note and the ring had been slipped on the table at a very opportune moment.

And the slide rule?

She couldn't imagine exactly when the slide rule had slipped out of its proud owner's pocket and fallen deep down between the cushions. But it had been after the last time she had seen him—and it meant that when he had last come to the house he had sat on the window-seat long enough for it to work its way out of his pocket. She sat there quite motionless for a long time while she thought about it.

CHAPTER 14

Soften the evidence.

The lecturer at Luston College of Technology rolled his eyes at his first visitor the next morning and said, "Hinton? He was another drop out, that's all, officer. We get them all the time."

"Do you know why?" asked Detective Constable Crosby.

"This isn't a kindergarten."

"No, sir, I'm sure."

"Hinton wasn't any different from all the others," he said irritably.

Crosby said he was sure he hoped not. "Did you make enquiries at the time, sir?"

"I didn't but the registrar will have done. He'll have had a grant, you know, and that will have had to be signed for."

"Quite so, sir." In an uncertain world the accounting profession was more certain than most. "Examinations, do you think it was, sir?"

"Examinations?" snorted the lecturer. "It's not examinations that they're afraid of. It's hard work."

"Can you tell me when he was last here?"

"That's not difficult. It'll be here in the register." He ran his thumb down a list. "Hinton, P. R., was here for the first two weeks of the summer term and not after that."

"Thank you, sir, you've been most helpful."

The courtesy appeared to mollify the lecturer. He opened up slightly. "He was supposed to be doing a dissertation, too, but he never handed it in. His home address? You'll have to ask the registrar for that too. I have an idea his family were abroad . . ."

* * *

Detective Inspector Sloan intended to concentrate first of all on the Mundill ménage. He began sooner than he expected when he bumped into Inspector Harpe of Traffic Division crossing the police station yard.

"Mundill?" Harry Harpe frowned. "I know the name."

"Demon driver?"

"No, it wasn't that." He frowned. "Mundill—let me think a minute." He slapped his thigh. "Got it!"

"Inner guidance?" suggested Sloan, not that Mundill had looked a drinker.

"Not that either." Harpe knew all the heavy drinkers for miles around. "He's an architect, isn't he?" Harpe nodded to himself with satisfaction. "Then he designed the multi-storey car park last year. He got some sort of architectural award for it. I met him at the official opening. You remember, Sloan, the mayor's car was the first one in."

Sloan had a vague memory of bouquets and mayoral chains and speeches and photographs in the local paper.

Harpe emitted a sound that for him was a chuckle. "But he couldn't understand the principle it was built on. I heard Mundill trying to explain it to him. The mayor couldn't see why the cars going up never met the cars going down."

"Two spirals," said Sloan immediately, "one within the other."

"Mundill gave it some fancy name and that didn't help the mayor one little bit."

"Double helix," supplied Sloan.

"That was it," agreed Harpe. "Mundill told him there was a well in Italy—at Orvieto, I think he said it was—that was built on the same principle. The donkey going down never met the donkey coming up. Clever chap. Not the mayor," he added quickly. "Mundill."

"It's a good car park," said Sloan.

And it was.

"Keeps the cars off the streets," agreed Harpe.

Sloan left Harpe while he was still thinking about the apotheosis of Traffic Division's dreams—totally empty roads.

When he got to his room Sloan picked up the telephone and made an appointment with Frank Mundill to go over to Marby during the morning to identify the boat on the beach.

He sat in front of the telephone for a long moment after that and then he dialled the County Police Headquarters at Calleford.

"I want a police launch," he said to the officer at the other end.

"Speak on."

"Strictly for observation."

"If you want the drug squad you've got the wrong number."

"I don't."

"That makes a change," said the voice equably.

"At least," said Sloan, "I don't think I do."

"Myself, I wouldn't put anything past the drugs racket."

"No." That was something he would have to think about. There was probably no one at greater risk than an addict—unless it was a pusher who double-crossed his supplier. Then revenge was simple and swift.

"This launch you want—where and when?"

"Off Marby. Round the headland. I shall be sending a constable up on the Cat's Back there to keep watch as well."

"Belt and galluses," remarked the voice.

"When do you want this observation kept?"

"Low tide," said Sloan without hesitation.

"Right you are. By the way," asked the voice, "what are they to observe?"

"A small fishing trawler called *The Daisy Bell,*" said Sloan, replacing the receiver.

Then, unable to put it off any longer, he knocked on the door of Superintendent Leeyes's office.

"Ha, Sloan! Any progress?"

"A little, sir." Intellectuals were not the only people to be troubled by the vexed relationship between truth and art. "Just a little."

"Know who he is yet?"

"Not for certain," said Sloan. He could have delivered a short disquisition, though, on the phrase "growing doubts."

Superintendent Leeyes waved a hand airily. "Find out what happened first, Sloan, and look for your evidence afterwards."

That wasn't what they taught recruits of Training School.

"We haven't got a lot of evidence to consider," said Sloan.

But it was too subtle a point for the superintendent.

"You've got a body," boomed Leeyes.

"Yes, sir." Dr. Dabbe's full post-mortem report had been on Sloan's desk that morning, too. It didn't tell him anything that the pathologist hadn't already told him, except that the young man had had a broken ankle in childhood, which might help.

In the end.

"With a piece of copper on it," Leeyes reminded him.

"Yes, sir." There were those who would call that an obol for Charon but they were not policemen. Sloan had a search warrant for Alec Manton's farm now. And he'd have to find out what Mr. Jensen at the museum had been up to. Things were obviously moving in the archeological world. Jensen had been out when he rang the museum.

"This ship under the water," said Leeyes abruptly. "Who does it belong to?"

"Strictly speaking," said Sloan, "the East India Company, I suppose."

"Ha!"

"But . . ."

"Not findings, keepings, eh, Sloan?"

"No, sir." Not even a bench of magistrates in the Juvenile Court would go along with that piece of childhood lore and faulty law. A roomful of lost property at the police station testified to the opposite too. He cleared his throat, and carried on, "Under the Merchant Shipping Act of 1894 . . ."

"Been at the books, have you, Sloan?"

"A wreck is deemed to belong to the owner . . ."

Come back, Robert Clive, all forgiven.

"And if the owner isn't found?" asked Leeyes.

"The wreck becomes the property of the state in whose waters she lies."

Full fathom five . . .

"And, sir, the goods discovered in a wreck . . ."

"Yes?"

"Can be auctioned."

"Who benefits?" asked Leeyes sharply. "Or does the Crown take?"

"The finder gets most of the proceeds." The superintendent's phrase reminded Sloan of a move on the chess-board.

The superintendent looked extremely alert. "That's different."

"Salvage," added Sloan for the record, "is something quite separate."

Leeyes's mind was running along ahead. "You're going to track this farmer down, aren't you, Sloan?"

"Oh, yes, sir." Alec Manton was high on his list of people to be seen.

So was a man called Peter Hinton.

Before that there was still some routine work to be done at the police station. He picked up the phone and quickly dialled a number.

"Rita, this is Detective Inspector Sloan speaking. I'd like to talk to Dr. Dabbe if he's not too busy."

"He isn't doing anyone now, Inspector, if that's what you mean."

That was what Sloan did mean.

"Hang on," said Rita, "and I'll put you through straightaway."

If a girl wasn't overawed by death, then neither doctors nor police inspectors were going to carry much weight . . .

"Dabbe here," said the pathologist down the telephone.

"We may," said Sloan circumspectly, "repeat may—just have a possible name for yesterday's body."

"Ah."

"There's a man called Peter Hinton who was last seen alive about two months ago at his lodgings in Luston."

"You don't," said the pathologist temperately, "get a great hue and cry from lodgings."

"If," advanced Sloan cautiously, "we had reason to believe that he might be our chap—your chap, that is—what would be needed in the way of proof?"

"His dentist," replied Dr. Dabbe promptly, "his dental records and a forensic odontologist. You'd be half-way there then."

"And the other half of the way?"

"A good full-face photograph that could be superimposed on the ones that have been taken here."

"I'll make a note of that," said Sloan.

He could hear the pathologist leafing through his notes. "Wasn't there a broken ankle in childhood, too, Sloan?"

"So you said, Doctor."

"Everything helps," said Dr. Dabbe largely, "and when they all add up, why then—well, there you are, aren't you?"

Which was scarcely grammar but which did make sense.

* * *

Detective Constable Crosby reported back to the police station with what he had gleaned about Peter Hinton and the death of Mrs. Mundill.

"I checked on her death certificate like you said, sir."

"Yes?" said Sloan. You couldn't be too careful in this game.

"Cachexia," spelt out Crosby carefully.

"And?" said Sloan. Cachexia was a condition, not a disease.

"Due to carcinoma of the stomach," continued Crosby. "It's signed by Gregory Tebot—he's the general practitioner out there."

Crosby made Collerton sound like Outer Mongolia.

Sloan assimilated his information about Peter Hinton too.

Soon he was telling the reporter from the county newspaper that he couldn't have a photograph of the dead man.

"We might get an artist's impression done for you," he said, "but definitely not a photograph."

"Like that, is it?" said the reporter, jerking his head.

"It is," said Sloan heavily. "But you can say that we would like to have any information about anyone answering to this description who's been missing for a bit."

"Will do," said the reporter laconically. He shut his note-book with a snap. If there was no name, there was no story. It was sad but true that human interest needed a name.

* * *

"So," he said, "there's just the widower . . ."

"Frank Mundill."

"And a niece . . ."

"Elizabeth Busby."

"And there was a boy-friend," said Sloan.

"Peter Hinton."

"It wouldn't do any harm," said Sloan slowly, "to check on Celia Mundill's will."

Crosby made an obedient note.

"Though," said Sloan irascibly, "what it's all got to do with the body in the water I really don't know."

"No, sir."

"And Crosby . . ."

"Sir?"

"While you're about it, we'd better just check that Collerton House wasn't where our body fell from. I don't think it's quite high enough. And there are shrubs under nearly all the windows. They wouldn't have healed."

In time Nature healed all scars but even Nature took her time . . .

* * *

Frank Mundill was ready and waiting at Collerton House when Sloan and Crosby arrived at the appointed time.

"We've just heard about the body that they've found in the estuary," he said. "Someone in one of the shops told my niece this morning."

Sloan was deliberately vague. "We don't know yet, sir, if there is any connection with it and the boat that was taken."

The architect shuddered. "I hope not. I wouldn't like to think of anyone coming to any harm even if they had broken in."

"The inquest will be on Friday," Sloan informed him. "We may know a little more by then."

Once over at Marby the architect confirmed that the boat beached beside the lifeboat had come from Collerton House.

"No doubt about that at all, Inspector," he said readily. "It's been in that boathouse ever since I was married and for many a long year before that, I daresay."

Crosby made a note in the background.

Mundill gave the bow a light tap. "She's good enough for a few more fishing trips, I should say. She's hardly damaged at all, is she?"

It was true. The boat had dried out quite a lot overnight and in spite of its obvious age looked quite serviceable now.

"I suppose," said Mundill, "that I can see about getting it back to Collerton now?"

"Not just yet, sir," said Sloan. "Our scientific laboratory people will have to go over it first."

Mundill nodded intelligently. "I understand. For clues."

"For evidence," said Sloan sternly.

There was a world of difference between the two.

"Then I can collect it after that?"

"Oh," said Sloan easily, "I daresay they'll drop it back to the boathouse for you."

"When?"

"Is it important?"

"No, no, Inspector, not at all. I just wondered, that's all. It doesn't matter a bit . . ."

* * *

Elizabeth Busby had hardly slept at all that night. And when she had at last drifted off, sleep had not been a refreshment from the cares of the day but an uneasy business of inconclusive dreams.

Waking had been no better.

She came back to consciousness with her mind a blank and then suddenly full recollection came flooding back and with it the now familiar sensation that she was physically shouldering a heavy burden. The strange thing was that this burden seemed not only to extend to an area just above her eyes but to weigh her down from all angles. At least, she thought, Christian in *The Pilgrim's Progress* only had a burden on his back—not everywhere.

Propped beside her bedside lamp was Peter Hinton's slide rule. She had considered this again in the cold light of day. And got no further forward than she had done the evening before. It really was very odd that Peter should have taken a water-colour painting of a beach and left his slide rule behind him.

As she had got dressed she viewed the prospect of another day ahead of her without relish. It wasn't that she wanted to spend her whole life wandering in the delicate plain called Ease, just that she could have done without its being spent so much in the Slough of Despond. She had eventually got the day started to a kind of mantra of her own. It was based on Rudyard Kipling's poem *If* and concentrated on filling the unforgiving minute with sixty seconds' worth of distance run . . .

The whole day stretched before her like a clean page. True, there were the finishing touches to be put to the spring-cleaning of the spare room and today was the day that the dustbin had to be put out, but otherwise there were no landmarks in the day to distinguish it from any others in an endless succession of unmemorable days.

By the time Frank Mundill had gone off in the police car to Marby she found herself with the spare room finished and the dustbin duly put out. That still left a great deal of the day to be got through and she turned over in her mind a list of other things that might be done.

For some reason—perhaps subconsciously to do with the finding of the slide rule—she was drawn back to the hall. Perhaps she would tackle that next in her vigorous spring-cleaning campaign. She stood in the middle of the space assessing what needed to be done. Quite a lot, she decided. This year's regular cleaning had completely gone by the board because of Celia Mundill's illness.

She stiffened.

She had resolved not to think about that . . .

Mop, duster, vacuum cleaner, step-ladder, polish . . . a list of her requirements ran through her mind before she went back to the kitchen to assemble them. All she needed was there save the big step-ladder. That lived in the shed and she would need it to reach the picture rail that ran round high up on the hall wall.

She dumped all her equipment in the middle of the floor and went off to the shed to get the step-ladder. It was leaning up against the wall in its accustomed place, standing amongst a conglomeration of gardening tools and old apple boxes. She moved the lawn-mower first and then a wheelbarrow. That left her nearer the steps but not quite near enough. She bent down to shift a pile of empty apple boxes . . .

It was curious that when she first caught sight of the shoe it didn't occur to her that there would be a foot in it. It was an old shoe and a dirty one at that and her first thought was that it was one of a pair kept there for gardening. That had been before she saw a piece of dishevelled sock protruding from it.

With dreadful deliberation she bent down and moved another layer of apple boxes.

A second shoe came into view.

It, too, had a foot in it.

Unwillingly her eyes travelled beyond the shoes to the grubby trousers above them. She could see no more than that because of the apple boxes. Driven by some nameless conception of duty to the injured, she lifted another round of apple boxes. The full figure of a man came into view then. He was lying prone on the floor. And she needn't have worried about her duties to the injured.

This man was dead.

CHAPTER 15

This is death without reprieve.

Unlike the sundial, Superintendent Leeyes did not only record the sunny hours. There were some stormy ones to be noted too.

"Dead, did you say, Sloan?"

"I did, sir."

"That means," he gobbled down the telephone, "that we've got two dead men on our hands now."

"It does, sir," admitted Sloan heavily. "There's no doubt about it either, sir. The local general practitioner confirms death."

After death, the doctor.

That was part of police routine too.

"One, two, that'll do," growled Leeyes.

"Sir?" Sloan had only heard of "One, two, buckle my shoe" and even that had been a long time ago now.

"It's a saying in the game of bridge," explained Leeyes loftily. "You wouldn't understand, Sloan."

"No, sir." Sloan kept his tone even but with an effort. There was so much to do and so little time . . . and something so very nasty in the woodshed.

"What happened this time?" barked Leeyes. "Not, I may say, Sloan, that we really know yet what happened last time."

"I should say that he was killed on the spot. In an unlocked garden shed, that is." It was Sloan's turn now to sit in the window-seat in the hall of Collerton House and use the telephone. A white and shaken Elizabeth Busby had led him there while

Frank Mundill stayed with Crosby and Dr. Tebot. "Hit on the head," said Sloan succinctly. "Hard."

Leeyes pounced. "That means you've got a weapon."

"There's a spade there with blood on it," agreed Sloan.

"But not fingerprints, I suppose," said Leeyes.

"I doubt it, sir," said Sloan, "though the dabs boys are on their way over now."

"Fingerprints would be too much to ask for these days."

Sloan was inclined to agree with him. Besides there was a pair of gardening gloves sitting handy on the shelf beside the spade. Sloan thought that the gloves had a mocking touch about them—as if the murderer had just tossed them back onto the shelf where he had found them.

"When did it happen?" snapped Leeyes.

"He's quite cold," said Sloan obliquely, "and the blood has dried . . ."

Congealed was the right word for the bloody mess that had been the back of the man's head but he did not use it.

A red little, dead little head . . .

"Yesterday, then," concluded Leeyes.

"That's what Dr. Tebot says," said Sloan, "and Dr. Dabbe's on his way." Too many things had happened yesterday for Sloan's liking.

"Yes, yes," said Leeyes testily. "I know he'll tell us for sure but you must make up your own mind about some things, Sloan."

He had.

"And don't forget to get on to the photographers, Sloan, will you?"

"I won't forget," said Sloan astringently.

"Who is he?" asked the superintendent. "Or don't you know that either?"

But Sloan did know that. "He's lying on his face, sir, and we haven't moved him, of course."

"Of course."

"But I think I know."

Leeyes grunted. "You'll have to do better than that before you've done, Sloan."

"Yes, sir." Truth's ox team had been Do Well, Do Better and Do Best. Sloan decided that he hadn't even Done Well let alone Better or Best.

"I think I've seen those clothes before, sir." And the body did look just like a bundle of old clothes. You wouldn't have thought that there was a man inside them at first at all . . .

"Ha!"

"Yesterday afternoon," said Sloan.

"That's something, I suppose."

"I think it's the man who found the body." Strictly speaking he supposed he should have said "the first body" now.

"The fisherman?"

"Horace Boller," said Sloan.

"The man in the boat," said Leeyes.

"The doctor here thinks it's him too, sir." Last seen, Sloan reminded himself, with Basil Jensen on board.

"So there's a link," said Leeyes.

"There's a link all right," responded Sloan vigorously. "He's got a barbary head in his pocket too."

"What!" bellowed Leeyes.

Sloan winced. They said even a rose recoiled when shouted at let alone a full-blown detective inspector.

"At least," declared Leeyes, "that means we're not looking at a psychological case."

"I suppose it does, sir." There was nothing the police feared so much as a pathological killer. When there was neither rhyme nor reason to murder, then logic didn't help find the murderer. You needed luck then. Sloan felt he could have done with some luck now.

"Have you," growled Leeyes, "missed something that he found, Sloan?"

"I hope not," said Sloan. But he had to admit that it had been his own first thought too.

"If he was killed because he knew something, Sloan," persisted Leeyes, "then you can find out what it was too."

"I'm sure I hope so, sir."

"He'd have known about *The Clarembald* being found," said Leeyes. "A fisherman like him . . ."

"He'd have known all the village gossip for sure, too, sir, a man like that."

"Dirty work at the crossroads there," said Leeyes, even though he meant the sea.

It had been highwaymen who waited at the crossroads to double their chances of getting a victim. They used to hang felons at the crossroads too in the bad old days. Perhaps the dirty work had sometimes come from hanging the wrong man. A police officer had an equal duty to the innocent and the guilty.

Then and now.

"Don't tell me either," said Leeyes tartly, "that men explore valuable wrecks for the fun of it."

Sloan wasn't so sure about that but he was concentrating on the bird in the police bush, so to speak.

"Boller wasn't a very attractive man," he said slowly. "Ridgeford said you had to watch him."

"Are you trying to suggest something, Sloan?"

"If he knew something that we didn't know he might have been—er—trying to put the pressure on a bit."

"Blackmail by any other name," trumpeted Leeyes, "smells just as nasty."

"And it's always dangerous." The blow that had killed Boller had been bloody, bold and resolute. Even peering over the apple boxes Sloan could see that. That's when he had seen the bulge in the man's pocket that had been the barbary head. Boller's own head hadn't been a pretty sight. Wet red—the poet's name for blood—it had been covered in.

"Was he destined for a watery grave, too, Sloan?"

"I'm sure I don't know that, sir. All I do know is that it was merest chance that he was found. The girl—Elizabeth Busby, that is—said that she only had that step-ladder out once in a blue moon. She was going to clean the hall and that's high, of course. Otherwise . . ."

"Otherwise," interrupted Leeyes tartly, "in a couple of months' time we'd have had an unidentified body on our hands, wouldn't we? Another unidentified body, that is."

"I think someone would have reported this man as missing," said Sloan. Ridgeford had mentioned that Horace Boller had a son with them on their first trip. He cleared his throat. "That means whoever killed him was pretty desperate."

"The blackmailed usually are, Sloan," said Leeyes with unusual insight. "Because they've always got the two things to worry about they stop thinking straight."

"What they've done and what someone's doing to them," agreed Sloan.

"Did he get there by water?" asked Leeyes.

"What—oh, I hadn't thought about that, sir. We'll have to see." There were so many things to see to now . . .

"We don't want two dinghies on the loose, do we?"

When Sloan got outside again Constable Crosby was standing on guard outside the shed door talking to a worried Frank Mundill.

"What is going on, Inspector?" said the architect wildly. "Why should this house be picked on for all these things?"

"The real reason," said Sloan, "is probably because it's big enough to have a shed and a boathouse that don't get used very often."

"That's very little consolation, I must say." He shuddered. "Ought you to search everywhere else?"

"No, sir, I don't think that will be necessary, thank you." Sloan had got some straight edges of his jigsaw on the board already. The death of Horace Boller—no, the killing of Horace Boller—was another piece. It might even prove to be one of the four most important pieces of all the puzzle—a cornerpiece.

Mundill ran a finger round inside the collar of his white turtleneck sweater. "It's an unnerving business, isn't it?"

"Nobody likes it, sir," agreed Sloan. He was glad about that. Sophisticated fraud sometimes wrung unwilling admiration from investigating officers, but murder was a primitive crime and nobody liked it. The killing of a member of a tribe by another member of the same tribe was an offence against society. And it meant that no one in that society was safe. Perhaps that was the real reason why the murder charge accused the arrested person not so much of a killing but of an offence against the Queen's Peace because that was what it was . . .

"That poor chap in there," said Mundill worriedly.

"Yes, sir." Sloan spared some sympathy for the dead man lying in the shed. But he carefully kept his judgement suspended. Horace Boller might have been lured to his doom by the murderer in all innocence but Sloan did not think so. There was a certain lack of innocence in Boller both as reported by Constable Ridgeford and observed by Sloan himself that augured the other thing.

"I could wish my niece hadn't found him too," murmured Mundill. "She's had a lot to put up with lately, poor girl. What with one thing and another I'll be glad when her mother and father get here."

Sloan nodded sympathetically. The scientists said that a cabbage cried out when its neighbour in the field was cut down so it was only right and proper that one human being should feel for another. The unfeeling and the too-feeling both ran into trouble but that was something quite separate.

"I hope Dr. Tebot's got her to go and lie down," said Mundill.

"I hope," said Sloan vigorously, "that he's done no such thing." Salvation lay in keeping busy and he said so, doctor or no.

"All right," said Frank Mundill pacifically, "I'll tell her what you said."

"And tell her," said Sloan, "that we'll be wanting a statement from her too . . ."

As Mundill went indoors Sloan advanced once more on the shed.

Both policemen peered down at the body.

"I'll bet he never knew what hit him," averred Crosby.

"No," agreed Sloan soberly.

Horace Boller did not necessarily have to have been blackmailing anyone. He might simply have learned something to his advantage that the murderer didn't want him to know about.

And so, in the event, to his ultimate disadvantage.

Something that a killer couldn't afford for him to know. That alone might be enough for a man who had killed once. Appetite for murder grew—that was something else too primitive for words. Having offended against society by one killing it seemed as if the next death was less important, and the one after that not important at all. By then the murderer was outside the tribe and beyond salvation too.

"We'd better get him identified properly," said Sloan mundanely.

"Yes, sir."

"What, Crosby," he asked, "can he have known that we don't know?" That was the puzzle.

Crosby brought his eyebrows together in a prolonged frown. "He could have seen that the boathouse had been broken into."

"And put two and two together after he found the body? Yes, that would follow . . ."

Blackmail, to be true blackmail, had to be the accusing or the threatening to accuse any person of a real crime with intent to extort or gain any property or valuable thing from any person.

Murder was a real crime.

"But he can't have known that the body in the water had been murdered, can he, sir?" objected Crosby. "I mean we didn't know ourselves until Dr. Dabbe said so. And we haven't told anyone."

"A good point, that." Sloan regarded the figure on the shed floor and said absently, "So he must have known something else as well . . ."

"Something we don't know?" asked Crosby helpfully.

"Or something that we do," mused Sloan. "He might have spotted that sand-hopper thing too."

"He knew about the sparling," said Crosby, "didn't he?"

Sloan squared his shoulders. "What we want is a chat with Mr. Basil Jensen."

* * *

Constable Brian Ridgeford was panting slightly. The cliff path—like life—had led uphill all the way and it hadn't been an easy one either. He'd left his bicycle down in the village. Now he was nearly at the top of the headland. He turned his gaze out to sea but it told him nothing. There was just an unbroken expanse of water below him. Far out to sea there was a smudge on the horizon that might just have been a container ship. Otherwise the sea was empty.

He settled himself down, conscious that he wasn't the first man to keep watch on the headland. Men had waited here for Napoleon to come—and Hitler. They'd lit armada beacons up here on the Cat's Back too as well as wrecking ones. From here the inhabitants of Marby might have seen the Danish invasion on its way.

"Keeping observation" was what Ridgeford would put in the book to describe his morning.

Watch and ward it used to be called in the old days.

It was much more windy up here than down in Marby village. He made himself as comfortable as he could in the long grass and turned his attention to Lea Farm. It was like a map come to life, farm and farmhouse printed on the landscape. He narrowed his gaze on the sheep-fold. Far away as he was he could see that the sheep-dipping tank was still full.

Ridgeford spared a thought for old Miss Finch. Difficult and dogmatic she might be but she hadn't been so silly after all. She probably had seen something happening on the headland. The theory of an accurate report book suddenly came to life. Write it down, they'd taught him . . . let someone else decide if what you'd written was valuable or not.

He swung his glance back in the direction of the sea. This time there was something to see. Round the coast from Marby harbour was coming a small trawler. Ridgeford got to his feet and walked farther up the headland to get a better view of it. As he did so he nearly tripped over a figure lying half hidden in the grass. It was a man. He was using a pair of binoculars and was looking out to sea so intently that he hadn't seen the approach of the policeman.

"Hullo, hullo," said Ridgeford.

The man lowered his binoculars. "Morning, officer."

"Looking for something, sir?"

"In a manner of speaking," he said, scrambling to his feet.

The trawler was forging ahead. Ridgeford noticed that it was keeping close inshore and that the other man could not keep his eyes off it. Ridgeford asked him his name.

"My name?" said the man. "It's Jensen. Basil Jensen. Why do you want to know?"

* * *

The general practitioner, Dr. Gregory Tebot, came out of Collerton House and joined Detective Inspector Sloan outside the shed while the various technicians of murder were bringing their expertise to bear upon the body inside it.

"She'll be able to talk to you now, Inspector," Dr. Tebot said. He was an old man and he looked both tired and sad.

"Thank you, Doctor," said Sloan.

"Shocking business," he said, pointing in the direction of the shed. "Are you going to tell the widow or am I?"

Death, remembered Sloan, was part of the doctor's daily business too. What he had forgotten was that Dr. Tebot would know the Bollers. "Tell me about him," he said.

"Horace? Not a lot to tell," said the doctor. "Didn't trouble me much."

"A healthy type then," said Sloan. Blackmail—if that was what he had been up to—was unhealthy in a different way.

"Spent his life messing about in boats," Dr. Tebot said. "Out of doors most of the time."

"Make much of a living?"

"I shouldn't think so. Picked up a little here and a little there, I should say. Mostly at weekends but you'd never know, not with Horace."

"Didn't give anything away then," said Sloan.

"He was the sort of man, Inspector," said the old doctor drily, "who wouldn't even tell his own mother how old he was." He nodded towards Collerton House. "Go easy with the girl if you can. She's had a packet lately, what with the aunt dying and everything."

"The aunt," said Sloan. A packet was an old army punishment. The "everything" was presumably a young man who had gone away.

"Hopeless case by the time I saw her," said Dr. Tebot. "The other doctor said so and he was right."

"What other doctor?"

"The one over in Calleford. I forget his name now. Mrs. Mundill was staying over there when she was first taken ill."

"I didn't know that."

"Nice woman," he said. "Young to die these days. Pity. Still, it happens."

"It happens," agreed Sloan. Perhaps they were the saddest words in the language after all.

"Pelion upon Ossa for the girl though."

Life was like that, thought Sloan. The agony always got piled on.

"She was very good with her aunt," said the doctor, "but she's nearly at the end of her tether now."

"I'll bear it in mind," said Sloan, but he made no promises. He had his duty to do.

He found Elizabeth Busby fighting to keep calm. "It was horrible, horrible."

"Yes, miss."

"The poor man . . ."

"He won't have felt anything," said Sloan awkwardly. "Dr. Tebot says he can't have done."

She twisted a handkerchief between her fingers. "Who is he? Do you know?"

"We think," said Sloan cautiously, "that it's someone called Horace Boller."

She sat up quickly. "Horace? But I saw him only yesterday."

"You did?"

"He rowed past while I was putting flowers on my aunt's grave. It's by the river, you see."

"You knew him then?"

"Oh, yes, Inspector." Her face relaxed a little. "Everyone who lives by the river knows Horace."

"He was," suggested Sloan tentatively, "what you might call a real character, I suppose?"

"He was an old rogue," she said a trifle more cheerfully.

Perhaps, thought Sloan to himself, that was the same thing . . .

"What did he say, miss?" he asked.

"Oh, he didn't say anything," she said. "He just rowed up river."

If Elizabeth Busby had noticed the broken boathouse doors so would Horace Boller. It was beginning to look as if he had taken the matter up with someone and that it had been a dangerous thing to do.

"You didn't see him again after that, miss?"

She shook her head.

"Nor near anything last night?" That was a forlorn hope. The garden shed was at the back of the house.

"No."

"Yesterday evening you and Mr. Mundill were both here?"

"I was," she said. "Frank wasn't. He'd gone to see someone about doing some measurements for an alteration to a house."

Sloan wrote down Mrs. Veronica Feckler's name and address.

"He went at tea time and stayed on a bit," she said.

"And you, miss?"

An abyss of pain yawned before her as she thought about the slide rule. "Me? I stayed in, Inspector. I didn't do anything very much." An infinite weariness came over her. "I just sat."

"And Mr. Mundill? When did he get back?"

"It must have been about eight o'clock. We had supper together." She looked up and said uncertainly, "When . . . when did . . ."

"We don't know for certain ourselves yet, miss," said Sloan truthfully. It was, he knew, the refuge of the medical people too. They professed that they did not know when they did not really want to say. There was no comeback then from the patient. And it was true sometimes that they did not know, but the great thing was that the point at which they did know was not the one at which they told the patient . . .

"Not, I suppose," she said dully, "that it's all that important, is it? What's important is that someone killed him."

"Probably," said Sloan with painful honesty, "what is important is why someone killed him."

He was rewarded with a swift glance of comprehension.

"For the record, miss," he went on, "I take it that to your knowledge Horace Boller did not come to the house?"

She shook her head.

"And that you heard and saw nothing?"

"Not a thing, Inspector." She lifted her face. "Not a thing."

"Thank you," he said quietly. "Now, miss, there are one or two things I want to ask you about a man called Peter Hinton . . ."

CHAPTER 16

Her tryal comes on in the afternoon.

At first it was impossible for Detective Inspector Sloan to tell if Elizabeth Busby was understanding the import of his questions.

She answered them readily enough.

She showed him Peter Hinton's note.

"It's in his handwriting, miss, I take it?"

"I hadn't thought it wasn't," she said uncertainly. "But I couldn't swear to it."

"Did he usually sign his name in full?"

"He hadn't—that is we didn't—write much. There was the telephone, you see."

"I see, miss."

"It was written with his pen," she said quickly. "He always wrote with a proper nib."

Later she showed him what was really troubling her. The slide rule.

Sloan regarded it in silence.

"He must have come back," she said, "and sat here after that last time."

"Could he be sure you wouldn't appear?" said Sloan.

"Towards the end," she said, a tremor creeping into her voice, "we never left Aunt Celia alone."

"So," said Sloan slowly, "if Mr. Mundill was down here in the hall you would be certain to be upstairs."

"Yes, that's right. We took it in turns."

"I see," said Sloan. Disquiet was the word for what he was feeling about Peter Hinton. "And you're sure your only disagreement the last time he was here was over whether your aunt should be in hospital?"

"Disagreement is too strong a word, Inspector." She'd recounted all the details of the last time she'd seen Peter Hinton. "Hospital was just something we talked about, that's all. Peter kept on suggesting it and we didn't want it. You can see that, can't you?"

"Yes, miss." He cleared his throat. "You don't happen to know if he ever broke his ankle, do you?"

"When he was seven," she said immediately. "He fell off a swing. Why do you ask?"

* * *

It is an undoubted fact that, once set in motion, routine gathers a momentum all of its own.

That was how it came about that Detective Inspector Sloan and Detective Constable Crosby, standing by a dead Horace Boller, were visited by a police motor-cyclist. He drew up before them, coming to a standstill with the inescapable flourish of all motor-cyclists, and handed over an envelope. Crosby tore it open.

"It's a copy of Celia Mundill's will, sir."

Routine took more stopping than did initiative. Surely there was a moral to be drawn there . . .

"Well?"

Crosby scanned it quickly.

Routine, thought Sloan, took on a certain strength too. Perhaps that was because it wasn't challenged often enough.

"It's short and sweet," said Crosby.

It seemed a very long time ago that Sloan had asked for it.

"She left," read out the constable, "a life interest in all her estate to her husband."

It occurred to Sloan that Mrs. Celia Mundill may very well have been in that delicate situation for a woman of being rather richer than the man she married. Certainly they had been living in her old family home and her husband's profession was conducted from her father's old studio.

"With everything," carried on Crosby, "to go to her only niece at his death."

"Including her share in the Camming patents," concluded Sloan aloud. Mrs. Mundill, then, had seen her role as a fiduciary one—a trustee for the past, handing down the flame to the future.

"And if the niece dies before the husband, then," said Crosby, "her sister collects."

"What else?"

"Nothing else," said Crosby.

"Date?" said Sloan peremptorily. There was a time to every purpose, the Bible said. The time for writing a will might be important.

Crosby looked at the paper. "April this year, sir."

The time had mattered then.

In olden days men would begin their last will and testament with their name and then add the prescient words "and like to die." The practice of medicine might not have amounted to very much in those days but at least then patients knew where they stood in relation to death, the great reaper. He wondered if Mrs. Celia Mundill had been "like to die" in April. If so she must have known it, too, and made her will.

And presumably her peace with the world.

Crosby started to fold up the paper again.

"Nothing," enquired Sloan appositely, "about remarriage?"

Wills were funny things. They lay dormant for years—like the seeds of some plants—and then something would stir their testators into activity again. Old wills would be torn up and new wills would be written. Or the testator died.

Crosby checked the will. "Nothing about the remarriage of the widower."

A time to get, and a time to lose, as Ecclesiastes had it.

No, not that.

A time to keep, and a time to cast away.

That was more like it.

Crosby folded the will neatly away. "Nothing for us in that."

"It doesn't appear to change anything," agreed Sloan cautiously.

That was the important thing with testamentary dispositions and crime.

"The widower's income doesn't change anyway," said Crosby.

"His death would matter to the girl," said Sloan. "That's all."

Crosby frowned. "Then she would scoop the pool, wouldn't she?"

"One day," said Sloan moderately, "she's going to be worth quite a lot of money." It didn't weigh against a bruised heart; he was old enough to know that.

"I wonder if that boy-friend of hers knew how rich before he ditched her," said Crosby.

In an ordinary man it would have been an unworthy thought; it was a perfectly proper one in a police officer.

"He didn't ditch her," said Sloan absently. He was sure about that now. "Somebody did for him. And put him in the river."

"Poor little rich girl," commented Crosby. He waved the will in the air. "What's this got to do with it all then, sir?"

"Probably nothing at all," said Sloan. The widower's income was assured, the niece's long-term future secure. "Money isn't everything, though," Sloan reminded the constable. It had been one of his mother's favourite sayings. It applied—with a certain irony—to some crime too.

"Comes in handy, though, doesn't it, sir. Money . . ."

"It's only one currency," insisted Sloan. "There are others."

There was fear—and hate.

With Horace Boller now it looked very much as if someone had been trading in silence. From the dead man's point of view it had been dearly bought. Sloan turned his attention back to the old fisherman. Not that looking at him was going to tell the police anything. What Sloan needed was a view into the man's mind before he had been killed.

"He found the body," mused Sloan aloud.

"He took us up river afterwards," said Crosby.

"He took Ridgeford out too," said Sloan, "to collect it."

"And that Mr. Jensen from the museum. Don't forget him."

"I haven't," said Sloan drily. "And I haven't forgotten *The Clarembald* either."

"He could have seen the boathouse doors, too," said Crosby. "We did."

"He did see Elizabeth Busby by the grave," said Sloan. "She said so."

"But," reiterated Crosby, "Boller didn't know that the man in the water . . ."

"Peter Hinton," said Sloan with conviction. He was sure of that now.

"Peter Hinton then had been pushed over the edge of somewhere, did he, so what was there for him to get so excited about?"

"Your guess, Crosby," said Sloan solemnly, "is as good as mine."

* * *

Interviewing Mrs. Boller had been an unrewarding business in every way, and now Sloan and Crosby were with Mrs. Veronica Feckler. It was impossible to tell whether she knew that she was being asked to provide an alibi for a man.

"Yesterday evening?" she said vaguely. "Yes, Mr. Mundill was here yesterday evening."

Detective Constable Crosby made a note.

"He came down after tea," she said.

"I see, madam."

Sloan was favoured with a charming smile. She was a personable woman and she knew it. "To measure up my cottage, you know."

"So we gather, madam."

She sketched an outline with a graceful hand. "I need another room building on. Frank—Mr. Mundill—he's an architect, you know . . ."

"Yes, madam." That much Sloan did know by now. Of the fire station, of the junior school, of Alec Manton's farmhouse and of a multi-storey car park.

And a multi-storey car park.

That was funny.

Frank Mundill hadn't mentioned that to Sloan. It had been Inspector Harpe who had told him about that multi-storey car park. Not Mundill. Even though he had got an award for designing it.

Mrs. Feckler said, "He's going to do my extension for me."

"How long was he with you, madam?" A thought was beginning to burgeon in Sloan's mind.

"Until just before supper." She wasn't the sort of woman who frowned but she did allow herself a tiny pucker of the forehead. "He left about half past seven. Is it important?"

* * *

It was strange, decided Elizabeth Busby, how heavy one's body could feel. She had almost to drag one leaden foot after the other. And yet she weighed the same—rather less, if anything—as she had done the day before.

When the inspector had left the house to go back to the shed she tidied away the cleaning things that she had brought out into the hall. There would be no more work done in Collerton House that day. She went into the kitchen and set about making coffee. That, at least, would be something useful to do and all those men out there would be glad of something to drink.

Time—even the most leaden-footed time—does eventually pass. And in the end the body of Horace Boller was borne away, the tumult and the shouting died and the photographers and the police—the captains and the kings—departed.

Frank Mundill came back indoors looking years older. "I'll be in my office," he said briefly, going upstairs.

She nodded. There suddenly didn't seem anything to say any more. She went and sat in the window-seat, her shoulders hunched up and unable to decide whether or not to take the tablets Dr. Tebot had left for her. He really did look as if a frock coat would have suited him, but he had been kind.

Even the hunching on the window-seat seemed symbolic. There was no leisurely resting in a chair for her today while she waited for Inspector Sloan to come back. The inspector had hinted—ever so delicately—but hinted all the same that he might have some more news for her later on and that he would return if he had.

"About Horace Boller?" she had asked.

"Not about Horace," he had replied.

Now she understood why Dante had had a place called Limbo in his portrayal of Hell . . .

It was quite a long time after that that she picked up the morning paper. It had been lying unregarded on the hall table since it had been delivered. It wasn't that she wanted to read it particularly, just that after a certain length of time she needed to do something with her hands. Not her head. That didn't take in any of what she was reading. Not at first, that is.

There is a certain state of alertness rejoicing in the grand name of thematic apperception which describes the attraction to eye and ear of items that the owner of that eye and ear is interested in. It explained how it was that Elizabeth Busby was able to read almost the whole paper without taking any of it in at all—until, that is, she turned to that page of the daily paper which dealt in—among other things—short items of news from the sale rooms.

"Bonington Sells Well" ran the headline.

"This previously unknown beach scene," ran the text underneath it, "thought to be of the Picardy coast and authenticated as being by Richard Parkes Bonington (1802–28), fetched the top price in a sale of nineteenth-century water-colours yesterday . . ."

Above the report was an illustration of the painting. It was the same one that had hung over the bed in the spare bedroom of Collerton House as long as Elizabeth could remember. It was the same one that Frank Mundill had said that Peter Hinton had asked for and been given.

She heard the tiniest sound on the stair and looked up quickly. Frank Mundill was standing there.

"Frank," she said at once, "you know that picture that Peter took . . ."

"What about it?" he said.

"It wasn't by Grandfather at all. Look!" She pointed to the newspaper. "It's here in the paper."

He strode over. "Let me see."

"There's a picture of it. It was worth a lot of money."

He said, "Well, it stands to reason that your grandfather had some good paintings, doesn't it? To copy."

That wasn't what was bothering Elizabeth. "Peter asked for it, you said."

Mundill frowned. "He did. It's the same one all right. Look, Elizabeth, I think there's an explanation for all this but there's something I would have to show you first."

"He hasn't been seen," she said dully. "The police said so. And they've asked me for a photograph."

"Come along with me," said Mundill. "I want you to see something. Something to do with Peter."

* * *

"There's no one here," said Detective Constable Crosby.

"Nonsense, man. Try again."

"I've tried," insisted Crosby. "The front door and the back. There's no answer."

"Mundill's car . . ."

"Not in the garage," said Crosby.

Detective Inspector Sloan took a swift look round the outside of Collerton House. There was no sign of life there at all.

"They've gone," said Crosby superfluously.

"Where?" barked Sloan.

"And why?" added Crosby. "I thought they knew we were coming back."

"They did," said Sloan gravely.

"Something's happened then."

"But what?" Sloan scanned the blank windows of Collerton House as if they could provide him with an answer. "And where the devil have they gone?"

"The river?"

"Not by car," said Sloan, adding under his breath a brief orison about that. The River Calle was too near for comfort. He would rather conduct searches on dry ground . . . "No, they've gone somewhere by car. Get on to Control, Crosby, and get that car stopped."

Crosby picked up the hand microphone in the police car and gave his message. Seconds later it came back to him and to every other police car in the county. "Calling all cars, calling all cars . . . Attention to be given to a dark blue Ford Zephyr, registration number . . ."

"It may be too late," said Sloan, although he didn't know for what.

"If seen," chattered the speaker, "stop and detain for questioning."

* * *

Frank Mundill drove over Billing Bridge and then gently along the Berebury road. He was quite quiet and Elizabeth didn't press him into speech. He drove carefully, glancing now and then into his rear-view mirror. What he did—or did not—see there evidently caused him a certain amount of satisfaction because he went on driving with unimpaired concentration.

She tried once to draw him out about the picture.

"Wait and see," he said.

"Where are we going?" she asked presently.

"Berebury," was all he said to that.

She tried once more to draw him out about the picture.

"All in good time, my dear."

Thus they came to Berebury. Reassured by yet another glance in his rear-view mirror, Frank Mundill steered the car towards the centre of the town.

"Frank, I don't understand . . ."

"You will. I've just got to park the car. It won't be difficult. It's early closing day."

He made for the multi-storey car park. Entrance was by ticket from a machine. He took the ticket and the entrance barrier automatically rose to let them through. He placed the ticket on the dashboard and nosed the car up to the first level. There were plenty of parking spaces there but he did not stop. Nor at the second level. It being a quiet afternoon there were no cars at all above the third level. The fourth level was empty too.

"Frank, where are we going? Why are we going right to the top? You must tell me."

"Upward and ever onward," he said, a smile playing on his lips now.

The car swept round the elliptical corner at the end of the building and up onto the highest level of all.

"Frank . . ."

"Soon be there," he said, accelerating. There were no other cars in sight now—just the bare ramps and parking places. He gave a swift tug at the steering wheel and soon they were in the open air again on the very top of the car park. He pulled the car neatly into a parking bay and got out.

Elizabeth followed him.

"This way," he said. "Do you know that on a clear day you can see Calleford?"

"I don't want to see Calleford," she said. "I want to know why the picture you said Peter wanted has been sold."

"You shall," he said softly. "You shall know everything soon. But first come this way . . ."

He walked away from the edge of the car park to the very centre.

"Follow me, Elizabeth. I designed this place, remember. I know what to show you . . ."

* * *

"Faster," said Sloan between gritted teeth.

Crosby changed up through the gears with demonic speed. "Which way?"

"Berebury," said Sloan. There was just the one hope that he was right about that.

The constable raced the car through the gates of Collerton House. With dressage and horses it was walk, trot, canter. With a souped-up police car it was a straightforward gallop from a standing start.

"Humpty-Dumpty sat on a wall," said Crosby. "Humpty-Dumpty had a great fall."

"Let's hope that we find the right wall," said Sloan tersely.

Crosby concentrated on keeping one very fast car on the

road. He took Billing Bridge faster than it had ever been taken before, narrowly avoiding caroming off the upper reaches of one of its stanchions.

"The car park in Berebury," said Sloan in a sort of incantation. "The multi-storey car park. It must be."

"What about it?" asked Crosby, cutting round a milk-float. The milkman was used to imprecations from faster drivers but not to being overtaken at that speed.

"It's the right height," said Sloan.

"So are a lot of things," said Crosby, crouching over the wheel as if he were a racing driver but in fact looking more like Jehu than any denizen of the race-track.

"Mundill designed it," said Sloan. "Two spirals round a central well. Come on, man, get a move on."

Crosby put his foot down still farther and the car ate up the miles into Berebury. They shot through the main street and swung round into the entrance of the car park. It did nothing for Sloan's blood pressure that they had to pause at the entrance like any shopping housewife to collect a ticket and allow the automatic barrier to rise.

"Hurry, man," urged Sloan. "Hurry!"

Crosby raced through the gears as fast as he could; the slope of the ramp needed plenty of power. The corner at the end, though, was tighter than any at Silverstone. He took it on two wheels.

"And again," commanded Sloan at the next level.

But they had lost speed on the way up. Crosby took the next bend more easily but at a slower rate.

"Keep going," adjured Sloan. He had his hand on the door catch.

They reached the top floor and came out into the sunshine. The sudden glare momentarily distracted both men but there was no disguising the dark blue Ford Zephyr standing in solitary state on the top platform or the two figures standing by the parapet of the central well. One of them had his arm round the other who appeared to be resisting.

"Stop!" shouted Sloan as he ran.

The man took a quick look over his shoulder and standing away from the other—a girl—vaulted lightly over the parapet.

CHAPTER 17

Here ends all dispute.

"I suppose," snorted Superintendent Leeyes, who was a sound-and-fury man if ever there was one, "that you're going to tell me that everything makes sense now."

"The picture is a little clearer, sir," said Detective Inspector Sloan. He was reporting back to Superintendent Leeyes the next morning, the morning after Frank Mundill's spectacular suicide over the edge of the parapet at the top of the multi-storey car park.

"Perhaps, then, Sloan, you will have the goodness to explain what has been going on."

"Murder, sir."

"I know that."

"More murder than we knew about, sir."

"Sloan, I will not sit here and have you being enigmatic."

"No, sir," said Sloan hastily. "The first murder wasn't of Peter Hinton at all. It was of Celia Mundill."

"The wife?" said Leeyes.

"The wife," said Sloan succinctly. "Frank Mundill wanted to marry Mrs. Veronica Feckler."

"Ha!" said Leeyes.

"So," said Sloan, "he set about disposing of his wife."

"He made a very good job of it," commented Leeyes.

"He nearly got away with it," said Sloan warmly. "He would have done but for Peter Hinton putting two and two together."

"So that's what happened, is it?"

"Elizabeth Busby tells me that Hinton was something of a

student of criminology, sir. His favourite reading was the Notable British Trials series."

"He suspected something?"

"We think so. Hinton wanted Mrs. Mundill in hospital."

"That wouldn't have done for a murderer," said Leeyes.

"No."

"So Peter Hinton had to go?" grunted Leeyes.

"Exactly." Sloan cleared his throat. "I—that is, we—think that he came back one day and challenged Mundill."

"And that was his undoing?"

"It was. He was a threat, you see, to the successful murder of Mrs. Mundill."

Talk of successful murders always upset the superintendent. "Do you mean that, Sloan?"

"I do, sir," said Detective Inspector Sloan seriously. "It was as near perfect as they come. We would never have known about the murder of Mrs. Mundill if he hadn't killed the young man too."

Leeyes didn't like the sound of that. "How perfect?"

"Arsenic, at a guess."

"You can't have a perfect murder with arsenic."

"You can if it's diagnosed and treated as cancer of the stomach," said Sloan.

"But what doctor would . . ."

"An old doctor who has had a letter from another doctor saying that that was what was wrong."

Leeyes whistled. "Clever."

"Very clever," said Sloan. "Each year the Mundills went at Easter to housekeep for a locum tenens. Mundill's sister is married to a single-handed general practitioner in Calleford. While Mrs. Mundill was there she had her first attack of sickness. The locum—a Dr. Penthwin—arranged for her to have an X-ray at Calleford Hospital."

"But it would be normal," objected Leeyes at once.

"Of course it would, sir," said Sloan, "but that doesn't matter."

"No?"

"All that matters is the letter that the Mundills bring back from Dr. Penthwin to their own doctor at Collerton, Dr. Gregory Tebot."

"A forgery?" said Leeyes.

"From start to finish," said Sloan who had seen it now. "Mundill writes it himself in the locum's name on professional writing paper. His brother-in-law knows nothing about it—neither does the locum, for that matter. Anyway Dr. Penthwin's soon gone. Dr. Tebot gets the letter which he thinks is from Dr. Penthwin and starts treating Mrs. Mundill for an inoperable cancer of the stomach."

"Most doctors would," agreed Leeyes reluctantly.

"Mundill sees that the doses of arsenic follow the course of the disease," said Sloan. "Peter Hinton spotted it was arsenic, I'm sure about that. He'd asked if her eyes kept on watering. That's what put us onto it too."

Leeyes grunted. "Mundill had long enough to look it all up in the books while he was over there."

"He'd even," said Sloan, "had long enough to go through the patients' medical records until he finds a letter with the wording pretty nearly the same as he wants."

"Clever," said Leeyes again. A whole new vista of medical murder opened up before him. "Has it been done before, do you think?"

"Who can say?" said Sloan chillingly. "Anyway, Dr. Tebot isn't going to start on fresh X-rays or anything like that, is he? He wouldn't see any need for them."

"The nearly perfect murder," said Leeyes.

"There was something else going for him, too, sir."

"What was that?"

"Celia Mundill didn't want to be cremated."

"And that suited the husband, I'm sure," said Leeyes.

"Cremation requires two medical certificates," said Sloan. "Burial only one." He'd lectured Crosby on the burial of victims of murder. A grave was the best place of all.

"The nearly perfect murder," said Leeyes again.

"He almost spoilt it, sir."

"How come?"

"Gilding the lily." It was surprising how often that happened with murderers. They wouldn't—couldn't—leave well alone.

"What lily?"

"The grave, sir. Mundill insisted on his wife being buried by the water's edge where the river floods."

"To help wash the arsenic away," said Leeyes. He cast his mind back. "That's been done before, hasn't it?"

"And to aid decomposition," completed Sloan. "I don't know how much it would have helped but I daresay he thought that if anyone got any bright ideas after he married Mrs. Feckler . . ."

Leeyes grunted. "He was going to marry her, was he?"

"He was," said Sloan. "On his wife's money. Financially he had nothing to lose by her death and a lot to gain."

"That's always dangerous," said the voice of experience.

"Mundill had a life interest in his wife's estate," said Sloan, "but he wanted a little capital too."

"Don't we all," said Leeyes.

"That," said Sloan manfully, "is why he sold a picture that wasn't his to sell."

"Ha."

"And blamed its disappearance on Peter Hinton."

"An opportunist if ever there was one," commented Leeyes.

"What put the girl's life in danger," said Sloan, "was her spotting the report of the sale in the daily paper."

It had been a close thing yesterday.

"If it hadn't been for that, eh, Sloan, Mundill might have got away with murder."

"I'm sure I hope not, sir," said Sloan.

"And the fisherman," said Leeyes. "Why did he have to go?"

"We think," said Sloan slowly, "that Boller must have been trying to apply a little pressure to Mundill."

"Why?"

"He wasn't a nice man," said Sloan obliquely. "He could easily have known all about Mundill's visits to Mrs. Feckler's cottage. He was about at all hours remember and not very scrupulous."

"He could have spotted that sand-hopper creature." Leeyes had seen the report on *gammarus pulex*.

"That was probably what took him up river the first time," said Sloan, "but I think it may have been his cousin Ted who gave him the real clue."

"Cousin Ted? You'll have to do better than that for the coroner, Sloan."

"Ted Boller is the village undertaker."

"What about it?"

"Mundill wouldn't have the coffin screwed down." The exhumation of Celia Mundill had begun that morning. A loose coffin lid had been the first thing that they had found. "Ted Boller didn't give it much thought but he did happen to mention it to his cousin."

"Horace Boller."

"Precisely, sir. It probably didn't mean anything to Horace either until he saw the girl beside her aunt's grave on Tuesday afternoon and realised how near the water it was."

"And so he put two and two together?"

"He probably just thought he would tackle Mundill about it."

Leeyes nodded. "By then, of course, Mundill will have got an appetite for murder."

"It grows," said Sloan. That was one area where policemen and psychologists were at one. An appetite for murder grew on itself. "Besides, sir, he couldn't risk Boller raising any doubts about Celia Mundill just when he was concentrating on keeping suspicion away from the body in the water."

"Talking of the body in the water, Sloan, what I can't understand is why Mundill broke the boathouse doors open. That just drew attention to the place."

"If," said Sloan, "anyone had found that body in there at any time without the outer boathouse doors having been prised open, they would know that Mundill had put the body there."

"And why not leave it there, Sloan, safely in the boathouse? Tell me that."

"Because, sir," said Sloan, "the girl's father was expected back from South America and he liked his little bit of fishing.

The boathouse would be the first place he'd make for. We were told that right at the beginning."

They'd been told almost everything; it was just a matter of sorting it all out. That was all . . .

"There's another thing, Sloan."

"Sir?"

"Those copper things that were found in their pockets . . ."

* * *

Brenda Ridgeford said, "I still don't understand about those copper things in their pockets, Brian."

"They were meant to put us off the scent," said her husband in a lordly fashion, "but they didn't."

"You mean *The Clarembald* wasn't anything to do with the murders?"

"Nothing," said Brian Ridgeford.

"But . . ."

"Mundill"—yesterday Brian Ridgeford wouldn't have dreamed of calling the architect anything except Mr. Mundill, but today the man was reduced to the ranks of common criminals—"simply took them from Mr. Manton's farm when he was over there."

Alec Manton was still entitled to be called "Mr."

Alec Manton and his amateur underwater research group had been investigating the trailings caught up by a trawler. That was how, explained Ridgeford, they had come on *The Clarembald.* They had proceeded to excavate the wreck.

In good faith and secrecy.

It had been the secrecy which had baffled Basil Jensen. When news of the great discovery was brought to the notice of an excited archeological world the name of the curator would be nowhere to be found.

"The biggest ever find on his patch," said Ridgeford, "and he wasn't being allowed a hand in it." He searched about in his mind for a parallel. "It would be like not letting me in on an armed raid in Edsway, Brenda."

"I don't want you in on any armed raids anywhere," said his wife. "Professional death comes in two ways, you know."

"They'd got a load of those copper ingots ashore," said the constable, "and we reckon Mundill spotted them one day at the farm. They didn't need keeping underwater, you see."

The sheep-dipping tank at Lea Farm had yielded a bizarre collection of wooden objects—a sea chest, a fid bound with lead, a table and something called a dead-eye.

"Used for extending the shrouds," Alec Manton had explained helpfully.

Brian Ridgeford had been no wiser.

"Poor Mr. Jensen," said Brenda Ridgeford. "Left out in the cold like that."

"Yes," said Brian Ridgeford uneasily. Far from leaving the museum curator out in the cold, he'd very nearly taken him into custody yesterday. "He's waving a protection order at Mr. Manton now."

"A piece of paper isn't going to save anything," said Mrs. Ridgeford.

Constable Ridgeford wasn't so sure about that. "With the strong arm of the law behind it . . ."

"There's ways round the strong arm of the law, Brian Ridgeford," she said provocatively, "I can tell you."

"That's as may be, my girl," he said with dignity, "but only when the law allows it."

* * *

"I suppose, Inspector," said Elizabeth Busby shakily, "that I have to thank you for saving my life."

"No, miss, you don't." Sloan was sitting on the window-seat in the hall of Collerton House again.

"He was going to kill me," she said, "because I knew about the picture."

"Murder's a dangerous game," said Sloan sententiously, "especially once the novelty's worn off."

"Poor, poor Aunt Celia."

Detective Inspector Sloan bowed his head in a tribute to a woman he had never seen alive. Dr. Dabbe was doing another post-mortem now—to make assurance doubly sure. Inquest-sure, too.

"The old, old story," she said bitterly.

"The eternal triangle," agreed Sloan. He'd read something once that put it very well . . . "The actors are, it seems, the usual three. Husband, wife and lover." It practically amounted to a prescription for murder. Aloud he went on, "And then murder once done . . ."

"Peter . . . poor Peter, too."

"He'd stumbled on your aunt's murder," said Sloan.

"He'd always been fascinated by crime," she said. "He read a lot about it."

"It was very clever of him."

"So he had to go, too," she said tightly.

"He had to be silenced," said Sloan. He coughed. "I take it that he'd have gone easily enough to have a look at the multi-storey car park if invited?"

"I did, didn't I?" She shuddered. "Frank sounded so reasonable and I really did think he had something there to show me. And there's no one up there on early closing day."

Sloan nodded. He could imagine Frank Mundill being plausible. "It was a perfect place," he said. "A double helix round a central light well, with a parapet at the top and a door at the bottom."

"A door with a key," she said.

"Mundill had a key, all right," he said. "And to the car park exit gate. He had done the original specification, remember. He had no problems in that direction. He had access to everything he wanted. He could come back at night for the body."

"It all fits, doesn't it?" she said.

All the pieces of the jigsaw were there now. Sloan would have to lock them together for his report but they were there. Elizabeth Busby didn't have to know about all of them. There was no point, for instance, in her being told about the blood that they'd found inside the light well of the car park, blood that wasn't Frank Mundill's. He did need to tell her about a photograph of Peter Hinton that had been superimposed on a photograph of a dead young man in Dr. Dabbe's mortuary.

And about a sure and certain dentist.

Sloan said nothing into the silence that followed his telling her.

Presently she said, "And Horace Boller?"

"He put two and two together about your aunt." Perhaps it hadn't been such a perfect murder after all. "He couldn't have known what really happened. Just that there was something wrong."

"And he paid the price."

"He knew what he was doing, miss." For Horace Boller anyway Sloan didn't feel too much pity . . .

Detective Constable Crosby was waiting in the car for him outside Collerton House. Sloan climbed into the passenger seat and shut the door with quite unnecessary vigour.

"A nasty case," he said.

Crosby started up the engine.

"Three murders," said Sloan. The only saving grace had been that a wicked man's cupidity had not succeeded . . .

"Mr. Basil Jensen," said Detective Constable Crosby, "wants us to meet him over at Marby."

Detection demanded many things of a man. A working knowledge of eighteenth-century ships was obviously going to be called for.

"All right," growled Sloan. "Get going then."

Crosby pulled the car away from the front door of Collerton House and settled himself at the wheel. He put a respectable distance behind him before he spoke.

"Sir . . ."

"What is it now?"

"What sits at the bottom of the sea and shivers?"

In the grip of powerful emotion and with an awful fascination Sloan heard himself saying, "I don't know what sits at the bottom of the sea and shivers."

"A nervous wreck."

About the Author

Catherine Aird is of Scottish descent, and lives now near Canterbury. She is the author of ten previous novels, including *Passing Strange, Some Die Eloquent,* and *Parting Breath.*

A-1

A1

AIRD, C
LAST RESPECTS

3

pp 124, 126 stained 4/89 [illegible]
OCT 25 1982

RODMAN PUBLIC LIBRARY
215 East Broadway
Alliance, OH 44601